Fading Stars
love, loss, and Liberation

Megha Saigal

BLUEROSE PUBLISHERS
India | U.K.

Copyright © Megha Saigal 2025

All rights reserved by author. No part of this publication may be reproduced, stored in a retrieval system or transmitted in any form or by any means, electronic, mechanical, photocopying, recording or otherwise, without the prior permission of the author. Although every precaution has been taken to verify the accuracy of the information contained herein, the publisher assumes no responsibility for any errors or omissions. No liability is assumed for damages that may result from the use of information contained within.

BlueRose Publishers takes no responsibility for any damages, losses, or liabilities that may arise from the use or misuse of the information, products, or services provided in this publication.

For permissions requests or inquiries regarding this publication, please contact:

BLUEROSE PUBLISHERS
www.BlueRoseONE.com
info@bluerosepublishers.com
+91 8882 898 898
+4407342408967

ISBN: 978-93-7018-991-1

Cover Design: Shubham Verma
Typesetting: Sagar

First Edition: April 2025

Acknowledgment

To my mom and dad— You've always seen something in me that I couldn't always see in myself. You believed I was made to change the world, even when I doubted it. Your love has been my anchor, your faith my guiding light. Thank you for teaching me that even when the world feels heavy, I am never alone.

To my friends—my chosen family— You are the ones who held me up when I couldn't stand on my own. You were my safe harbor in the storm, the hands that pulled me back to shore when I was drowning. Your laughter, your love, and your unwavering belief in me have been the glue that held me together. I wouldn't be here without you.

To my family— You've been my constants, my cheerleaders, my home. Thank you for standing by me, even when I didn't know how to ask for help. Your love has been my foundation, and your support has carried me through my darkest days.

And to everyone who has ever felt lost, broken, or unsure of where to turn— This book is for you. For the moments when you felt like giving up, for the nights when the weight of the world felt too heavy to bear, and for the mornings when you found the strength to try again. You are not alone. Your story matters, and your journey is worth every step.

This book is a love letter to resilience, to healing, and to the quiet, unshakable hope that lives inside all of us. Thank you for letting me share it with you.

Preface

"Woh afsana jise anjaam tak laana na ho mumkin,
Usay ek khoobsurat mod dekar chhodna achha..."
— Sahir Ludhianvi

Some love stories aren't meant to last forever. Some burn so fiercely in the beginning that they leave behind nothing but embers, reminders of what once was. Love, we are told, is meant to endure—it is meant to be patient, unwavering, selfless. But what happens when love asks for too much? When it demands pieces of you until you no longer recognize the person staring back in the mirror?

Fading Stars isn't a love story where misunderstandings are resolved, pain is overcome, and love conquers all. It's a story of love, yes—but also of its slow, painful unraveling. It's about the kind of love that begins as a spark and turns into a cage, the kind that convinces you to stay long after you should have walked away.

We are taught that love requires sacrifice, that patience and perseverance can mend even the most fractured relationships. But what happens when staying feels like losing yourself? When the person who once made you feel whole is the very reason you are falling apart?

This book is Maya's journey—her realization that love alone cannot fix someone who refuses to change. It is about the weight of emotional manipulation, the quiet destruction of self-worth, and the painful, necessary decision to choose herself. *Fading Stars* is not about love winning—it is about Maya winning. It is about walking away, even when it feels impossible, even when every part of her still aches for what once was.

This is a book for anyone who has ever felt trapped in a love that hurt more than it healed. For those who have questioned their own reality, doubted their strength, or struggled to let go. And for those who have finally found—or are still searching for—the courage to leave.

Because not all love stories are meant to last. Some are meant to teach us how to save ourselves.

Contents

1. Maya Walks Away 1
2. The Weight of Freedom 7
3. Maya's Realization 12
4. The Freedom of Letting Go 17
5. The Shattered Illusion 23
6. The Return of Vivhaan—And
   the Ghosts of Their Past 31
7. The Echo of the Past 35
8. The Other Side of the Story 40
9. A Journey Back to Maya's Self 46
10. Vivhaan's Struggle for Control 50
11. Vivhaan's Return 58
12. The Weight of the Past 62

13. The Road to Rediscovery 69
14. The Calm After the Storm 75
15. The Unexpected Encounter 82
16. The Ripple Effect 88
17. The Strength of Silence 93
18. Redemption Journey 98
19. The Final Goodbye 105
20. Moving Forward 111
21. What Lies Ahead 115

Epilogue 119

Maya Walks Away

Maya pressed herself against the wall, her breath hitching as Vivhaan stumbled closer. The air between them was thick with tension and the sharp, acrid smell of alcohol. His eyes were bloodshot, wild—the man she once loved was now unrecognizable.

Her mind flashed back to the first time she had seen him like this, months ago, when the drinking had started to spiral out of control. Back then, she had told herself it was just stress, that he would snap out of it. But now, as he loomed over her, his breath hot and uneven, she realized how wrong she had been. The man who had once made her feel safe now made her feel like a stranger in her own home.

"You're not leaving me!" he snarled, his voice low and menacing.

"I can't do this anymore, Vivhaan," she said, her voice trembling but firm. "You're drunk. Please, just let me go."

Her heart ached as she spoke the words, each one a dagger to the love she had once felt for him. She had spent years convincing herself that she could fix him, that her love would be enough to pull him out of the darkness. But now, as she stood there, her back pressed against the wall, she realized the truth: she couldn't save him. Not if it meant losing herself in the process.

"Let you go?" He laughed darkly, his steps unsteady yet purposeful. "You don't get to decide that, Maya. You don't get to walk away after everything I've done for you."

Her back hit the corner of the room, the cold plaster sending a shiver through her. She held her hands up, a feeble attempt to create distance between them. "I'm not doing this because I hate you," she whispered. "I'm doing this because I can't survive like this."

His expression twisted, the words like gasoline on an open flame. In a flash, his hand shot out, wrapping around her throat.

"Survive?" he hissed, his grip tightening. "You think you're the victim here? You think I'm the monster?"

Her hands clawed at his wrist, her nails digging into his skin as she struggled for air. "Vivhaan... please..." she gasped, her vision blurring. The world around her began to spin, the edges darkening. For a terrifying moment, she felt her body go limp, her mind slipping into a void. And then, just as quickly, the pressure released.

She collapsed to the floor, coughing and gasping for breath, her trembling hands clutching her neck. The sound of her ragged breaths filled the room as she slowly regained awareness.

"Maya..." Vivhaan's voice was softer now, horrified. He stumbled back, his hands shaking. "I didn't mean to—"

She looked up at him, her face pale but her eyes blazing with something new—something that hadn't been there before. Not fear. Not sorrow. But resolve.

"You almost killed me," she said, her voice hoarse but steady.

"No, no, no," he stammered, shaking his head. "I wasn't... I didn't mean to hurt you. Maya, I swear—"

"Stop," she snapped, cutting him off. She pulled herself to her feet, her body shaking but her voice unwavering. "Just stop."

Vivhaan reached out, his face twisted with desperation, but she stepped back, her glare stopping him in his tracks. "I loved you," she said, her voice breaking. "I gave you everything I had. And this is what you've turned me into—a shell of myself, terrified of the man who was supposed to protect me."

"I can change," he pleaded. "I'll stop drinking. I'll go to therapy. I'll fix this. I'll fix us!"

She laughed bitterly, the sound cutting through the tension like a blade. "Fix us? There is no us anymore, Vivhaan. You killed it. You killed the love, the trust, the hope."

Her voice trembled as she continued, but she didn't let the tears fall. Not this time. "You don't deserve me. You don't even see me. I'm not just some punching bag for your frustrations or a caretaker for your demons. I am done being your victim."

She turned and grabbed her bag, her movements swift and determined.

"Maya, please..." he begged, his voice breaking.

Her hand paused on the doorknob, but she didn't turn around. "Get help, Vivhaan. Not for me. For yourself. Because if you don't, this will be the end of you, too."

With that, she opened the door and stepped out into the hallway, her chest heaving. The air outside felt cold and sharp against her skin, but it was a relief compared to the suffocating weight of the apartment.

*****

How did it come to this? she asked herself. She had asked that question so many times over the years, but this time, it felt different. This time, she had the answer. She wasn't walking away out of anger or resentment—she was walking away because she finally understood the depths of the darkness she had been pulled into.

Her mind flashed back to what had happened. His hands around her neck, his grip tightening as her breath caught in her throat. The fear had consumed her, raw and paralyzing, as she clawed at his hands, desperate for air. In that moment, she had seen the person she loved become a stranger—a stranger capable of breaking her completely.

She wasn't just walking away for herself. She was walking away to survive. To reclaim the parts of her he had tried to erase, and to ensure that no one would ever make her feel that kind of terror again.

For years, she had been stuck in a cycle with Vivhaan. A beautiful, intoxicating cycle of love, pain, and promises. But now, those promises felt like lies. His apologies no longer carried weight; his empty words just echoed in the quiet corners of their home. Every time he swore things would change, she wanted to believe him. She needed to. But this time, her heart no longer wanted to listen.

Inside, Vivhaan sat on the couch, his thoughts a blur. He was still trying to piece together what had just happened. They'd had their arguments before, but this felt different. More final. His chest tightened as he ran his hand through his hair. He needed to fix things, to smooth it all over like he always did. He had to.

He stood up, pacing, a knot of anxiety growing tighter in his stomach. **What was going on?** Wasn't this just a bad patch? He thought they were getting through it. His mind circled around the small arguments, the things he'd said in anger. But it was all just a misunderstanding, wasn't it?

*****

Maya leaned against the wall of the building, her legs trembling. Her phone buzzed, startling her out of her daze. She fumbled for it, her hands still shaking. Aisha's name flashed on the screen.

"Hello?" Maya said, her voice barely audible.

"Maya?" Aisha's voice was sharp, full of concern. "What happened? Are you okay?"

"I left him," Maya whispered, tears spilling down her cheeks. "He... he almost..."

Her voice broke, and she couldn't finish the sentence.

"I'm coming to get you," Aisha said firmly.

"No," Maya said quickly, wiping her tears. "I just need a moment. I'll call you when I'm ready."

"Okay," Aisha said softly. "But promise me you'll stay somewhere safe. I'm here whenever you need me."

Maya nodded, even though Aisha couldn't see her. "I will. Thank you."

She hung up and closed her eyes, letting the cold air steady her. The ache in her neck was a reminder of what she was walking away from, but also of the strength it had taken to finally leave.

For the first time in years, she felt a glimmer of hope.

She wasn't just walking away. She was walking toward freedom.

The Weight of Freedom

Maya's apartment felt cold, even with the warmth of the evening air drifting in through the open window. Maya stood motionless in the doorway, her hand resting on the edge of the frame as she surveyed the empty space before her. It was a simple one-bedroom with bare walls and simple furniture. The house that she had bought before she shifted in with him as an investment on his insistence. It wasn't much, but it was hers.

The apartment was eerily quiet, save for the hum of the ceiling fan overhead. Maya sat cross-legged on the couch, her fingers playing absently with the fraying edge of a throw pillow. Her bag sat slumped against the wall, half-open, its contents spilling out like an accusation. She hadn't even packed it properly—a couple of outfits, her toothbrush, her journal. It was as if part of her hadn't truly believed she'd go through with it.

She glanced around the apartment again, trying to ground herself in her new reality. It was small, cold, impersonal—a far cry from the warmth of the home she had shared with him.

Stop thinking about him, she scolded herself, but the memories flooded in anyway.

The text she had sent him before she left echoed in her mind: *I'm just... done.* It had taken her ten minutes to write those three words. Ten minutes of pacing back and forth, her thumb hovering over the screen, her mind wrestling with every ounce of doubt she had.

Her phone buzzed on the cushion next to her, jolting her from her thoughts. She grabbed it quickly, her heart racing—but it wasn't him. It was just a notification from some app she barely used. She sighed, setting the phone down, disappointment tightening her chest.

What went wrong?

The question swirled in her mind, relentless and suffocating. She hugged her knees to her chest, resting her chin on them, and stared at the floor.

*****

Maya's thoughts drifted to the early days, back when things had been easy, when laughter had come naturally, and love hadn't felt like a battleground. She could still hear his voice, teasing her as she struggled to parallel park on their second date.

"Careful, Maya, you're about to kill that poor tree," he had said, smirking as he leaned against the passenger door.

"Shut up," she'd snapped, but she was laughing, her cheeks flushing with both embarrassment and joy.

"You know, I could always park it for you," he had offered.

"I don't need your help!" she had declared, finally getting the car into the spot—crooked but parked.

He had clapped, a playful grin lighting up his face. "See? That's why I like you. Stubborn as hell."

Her lips quivered at the memory, a bittersweet ache spreading through her chest. *When did we lose that version of us?* she wondered.

*****

The fights had started small. The first one she could remember was about his drinking.

"Do you really need another beer?" she had asked, her tone more curious than confrontational.

He had shrugged, opening the fridge. "It's just one. What's the big deal?"

"It's not about the beer, Vivhaan. It's about... I don't know, balance," she had tried to explain.

"Balance?" He had laughed, but there was an edge to it. "Maya, it's a drink, not a philosophy class."

She had let it go that night, but the unease had settled in, growing heavier with each argument that followed.

Maya wiped at her eyes, realizing that the tears had started to fall again. She stood up, pacing the small living room, trying to shake off the weight of the memories. Her phone caught her eye, and before she knew it, she was scrolling through her contacts. She paused when she reached Tara's name.

Tara always knew what to say. She'd probably tell her to breathe, to take it one day at a time, to remind her that leaving was the right thing to do. But as her finger hovered over the call button, doubt crept in.

"What if she thinks I'm weak?" Maya whispered to herself. "What if she thinks I should've stayed and tried harder?"

Her thumb moved away from the screen, and she let the phone drop onto the couch.

*****

Maya sat back down, pulling her knees up to her chest again. Her thoughts spiralled deeper, and she began to question herself.

"Was it me?" she muttered aloud, her voice trembling. "Was I the problem?"

She thought about all the times she had begged him to change, to try, to care. She thought about the nights she had cried herself to sleep, wondering if she was asking for too much.

"Maybe I was too demanding," she whispered, her voice barely audible. "Maybe I didn't give him enough space. Maybe... maybe I was the bad person in this relationship. His villain."

The word hung in the air, heavy and cruel. She shook her head, tears streaming down her face. "No, that's not fair. I tried. I *tried*."

But had she? Had she really done enough?

Her mind drifted back to one of their last good days—a lazy Sunday morning. She had been curled up in bed with a book, and he had come in with two cups of coffee.

"Look at you, all cozy and intellectual," he had teased, setting the mug on her nightstand.

"Somebody has to keep the brain cells alive in this relationship," she had shot back, smiling.

He had laughed, pulling her into his arms. "God, I love you," he had said, and for a moment, everything had felt perfect.

"Where did that man go?" Maya asked herself, her voice breaking.

*****

The tears came in waves now, unstoppable and raw. She cried for the man she had once loved, for the future they had dreamed of, for the woman she used to be before all of this had chipped away at her.

She lay down on the couch, pulling a blanket over herself. Her body trembled as she cried, her sobs echoing in the empty apartment. She cried until there were no tears left, until the exhaustion overtook her.

As she drifted off to sleep, her mind whispered one last, haunting question:

What if I never find love like that again?

Maya's Realization

Maya's morning began with a phone call.

Not the kind of call that flips your world upside down in an instant, but the kind that sneaks in and quietly rearranges the pieces of your life. The kind you don't expect, even when some part of you knew it was coming all along.

"Hi, Maya. It's Vivhaan's mom," the voice on the other end said. The words were calm, measured, but they carried the weight of inevitability. Maya's stomach tightened. She didn't need to hear the rest to know it was important.

"Vivhaan's in rehab," his mother continued after a pause. "It'll be three months. I thought you should know."

Three months.

The words echoed in Maya's mind, settling heavily in her chest. Relief washed over her first—a wave so unexpected it left her breathless. She didn't fully understand why at first, but as she sat there, phone pressed to her ear, she realized it wasn't about him getting better. It was about her. For the first time in years, she had space. Three months of silence. Three months to breathe. Three months to figure out what life could look like without him.

His mother's voice softened, tinged with a mix of hope and expectation. "Don't worry, Maya. He'll come out of this better. You'll see."

Better? Maya wasn't sure she cared anymore.

That night, she lay on her bed, staring at the ceiling. The city lights outside her window cast soft, shifting patterns across the walls, but her mind was fixed on the past. Three months, she thought again. It wasn't a lot of time, but it felt like a chance— a fleeting window to rediscover herself.

Yet beneath the relief was grief. Not for what had been lost, but for what she had given away.

*****

The Rehab

Vivhaan sat in the sterile confines of the rehab room, a place stripped of distractions, excuses, and pretences. The walls were a neutral, unremarkable shade, and the silence was heavy—almost oppressive. He hated it. But deep down, he knew he needed it. This wasn't punishment; it was a reckoning.

For the first time in years, he was alone with himself. No buzzing phone. No bottle to dull the ache. Just him and the unfiltered truth. And the truth was ugly.

Regret hit him like a freight train, relentless and unyielding. He had spent so long convincing himself that his actions were justified—that the drinking, the anger, the sharp words were temporary, controllable. But here, under the unforgiving light of clarity, those illusions crumbled.

It wasn't the world that had done this. It wasn't Maya. It was him.

*****

Their Love Story

It had begun like a dream.

Vivhaan remembered the first time he truly noticed Maya. They were sitting at a café with a group of friends, laughing over something trivial. She wasn't loud or attention-seeking, but there was something about her presence—a quiet energy that made her magnetic. Her laugh was unguarded, her smile disarming. In that moment, she had felt like sunlight breaking through a cloudy sky.

They had met on a dating app—an unremarkable start for something that had felt extraordinary. Their conversations had flowed effortlessly, text after text, voice note after voice note. She had a way of making him feel seen, like his flaws didn't define him.

Their first date wasn't extravagant. A simple picnic outside his building, sandwiches and cheap wine under a blanket of stars. It was ordinary, yet it felt like magic. Maya had a gift for turning the mundane into something memorable.

For a while, they were happy. Truly happy. Maya had brought light into his life, and he had clung to it, desperate to hold on. But the cracks had been there from the start, slow and subtle. The cracks were him.

Vivhaan had always struggled with his insecurities, but he thought he could hide them. He drank to silence the voices in his head—the ones that told him he wasn't enough. At first, it was a drink here and there, harmless in his mind. But it didn't take long for the drinking to spiral into something darker, something he couldn't control.

Maya saw it, of course. She always saw him. In the beginning, she tried to help. She held him through the bad nights, forgave him for the harsh words, and patched up the pieces he had broken. But over time, her resilience started to wear thin. Every broken promise, every night spent waiting for him to come home sober, chipped away at the love they had built.

*****

Maya's Realization

Maya lay back in bed, Vivhaan's mother's words still echoing in her mind. She thought of Vivhaan—not the man he had become, but the man he used to be. The man she had fallen in love with. And then, the man who had chipped away at her confidence, her joy, her peace.

She thought about the woman she used to be. The one who laughed freely, who believed in love as an unshakable force. Loving Vivhaan had changed her. It had made her question her worth, her instincts, her boundaries.

For so long, she had tried to hold on. She had clung to the hope that things could go back to the way they were. But now, she realized something she had been too afraid to admit: she had been losing herself with every chance she gave him.

The grief was still there, but it wasn't the kind that left her paralyzed. It was quiet, steady, like the tide pulling back after a storm. It wasn't just about losing him. It was about finding herself again.

Maya wasn't angry anymore. She wasn't even heartbroken. She was simply done. And for the first time in a long time, that felt like freedom.

The Freedom of Letting Go

Maya stood at the edge of her balcony, the city lights sprawling beneath her like tiny flickers of hope. The view hadn't changed, but the way she saw it had. This was the same city she had once explored with Vivhaan—the late-night drives, the impromptu dinners, the stolen moments of joy. Now, it felt like a new place, a new world waiting to be discovered.

The decision to leave him lingered in her chest, pressing in like a heavy stone, but underneath it, there was something unfamiliar—lightness. The cool night breeze brushed against her face, lifting stray strands of her hair. She closed her eyes, inhaling deeply, as if every breath could cleanse her of the past.

As she gazed out at the skyline, memories of Vivhaan began to surface—not the fights or the lies, but the moments that had made her fall in love with him.

*****

Flashback: The Day They Decided to Move In

"Are you sure about this?" Maya had asked, sitting cross-legged on the floor of his apartment, surrounded by empty pizza boxes and paint swatches.

Vivhaan leaned back against the couch, a playful grin on his face. "Maya, we've spent the last three months practically living together anyway. This just makes it official."

She bit her lip, glancing at the swatches in her hand. "And you're okay with me turning your 'bachelor pad' into something that looks... less like a bachelor pad?"

He laughed, reaching over to tuck a strand of hair behind her ear. "As long as you're here, you can paint the walls neon green for all I care."

She rolled her eyes. "You'd regret that in a week."

"Maybe," he admitted, his expression softening. "But I wouldn't regret us. Not for a second."

The warmth in his voice had made her heart flutter, and in that moment, everything had felt right.

*****

The Present

Maya shook her head, as if trying to clear the memory. That version of them—the hopeful, wide-eyed couple planning a future together—felt like a different lifetime.

Her phone buzzed on the balcony railing, jolting her from her thoughts. It was Tara, her best friend.

"Get dressed," Tara's voice chirped through the speaker. "We're going out tonight. And don't you dare say no."

Maya smiled faintly. "It's been a long day, Tara. Can't we just stay in?"

"Oh no, you've stayed in enough. We're going to that rooftop bar you love. I'll pick you up in 30 minutes. Be ready."

Tara didn't wait for a response before hanging up, leaving Maya staring at her phone. For a moment, she hesitated. The thought of being surrounded by strangers, pretending she was okay, felt daunting. But then she caught her reflection in the glass door—a woman she barely recognized.

*****

Flashback: The First Impromptu Road Trip

"Let's just go," Vivhaan had said, his eyes sparkling with mischief as he dangled his car keys in front of her.

Maya looked up from her laptop, incredulous. "Go where?"

"Anywhere," he said, pulling her to her feet. "Come on, you've been staring at that screen for hours. Let's drive until we find something worth stopping for."

She laughed, shaking her head. "You're impossible, you know that?"

"And you're overthinking," he countered, guiding her toward the door.

An hour later, they were parked by a quiet lakeside, the city far behind them. They sat on the hood of his car, sharing a bag of chips and watching the sun dip below the horizon.

"I don't think I've ever felt this free," she had admitted, leaning her head on his shoulder.

"Get used to it," he had replied, his voice low and steady. "Because that's how I want you to feel every single day—with me."

*****

The Rooftop Bar

The city stretched out in every direction, glittering under the night sky. Maya and Tara sat at a table near the edge, a soft hum of music and conversation filling the air.

"Here's to new beginnings," Tara said, raising her glass of sparkling rosé.

Maya hesitated before clinking glasses. "To not making the same mistakes twice," she added with a smirk.

"That's the spirit!" Tara laughed, her eyes twinkling. "I'm telling you, Maya, this is your time. No more sulking. You're free now, and the world is full of possibilities."

Maya smiled, taking a sip of her drink. "I don't even know what freedom feels like anymore. But sitting here... it's a start."

*****

Flashback: Their First Dance at Home

It had been a rainy evening, the kind where the city seemed to slow down. They were in Vivhaan's kitchen, cooking a chaotic dinner that had already gone wrong twice.

"This is a disaster," Maya groaned, holding up a soggy piece of pasta.

Vivhaan grabbed her hand, spinning her around suddenly. "Then let's forget the pasta and dance instead."

"Dance? Here? Now?" she laughed, trying to pull away.

"Why not?" he said, pulling her closer. He began humming a tune, his steps exaggerated and clumsy.

Maya couldn't help but laugh, letting him guide her around the tiny kitchen. By the time the song in his head ended, they were both breathless, leaning against the counter and grinning like fools.

*****

The Present

Maya sat at the rooftop bar, sipping her drink as the music swirled around her. The flashbacks came and went, leaving behind a bittersweet ache. She had loved Vivhaan deeply, and in those early days, he had loved her too. But love had twisted into something else, something that left her doubting herself, apologizing for things she hadn't done, and losing sight of who she was.

Now, sitting here, she felt the first flickers of something new—clarity.

*****

Later That Night

Back on her balcony, Maya gazed out at the city lights again. The memories still lingered, but they no longer consumed her. She thought of Vivhaan—not with anger, but with acceptance. He had been a part of her story, a chapter that had shaped her. But he wasn't her ending.

Her phone buzzed on the table behind her. A message from Tara: "How's my favorite artist tonight? Ready for our hike tomorrow?"

Maya smiled as she typed back: "More ready than ever. Let's do this."

As she hit send, she glanced back at the city one last time before stepping inside. The future was uncertain.

The Shattered Illusion

Maya once believed that love was enough to heal even the deepest wounds. With Vivhaan, she had clung to that belief, pouring every ounce of her energy into saving him from his demons—his insecurities, his temper, and his relationship with alcohol. But over time, she realized that her love wasn't healing anything; it was only breaking her further.

Vivhaan's drinking had started small—occasional drinks at dinners, celebratory toasts at parties—but slowly, it spiraled into something darker. He would stumble home late at night, his words slurred, his temper short. At first, Maya didn't mind. She chalked it up to stress, to the pressures of his work and family. She stayed up with him when he was low, holding him when he cried, comforting him when he promised to quit. He was like a child, desperate for attention, and she gave it unconditionally. But the more she gave, the more he took. And in return, he gave her control—tight, suffocating control.

The First Signs

The signs were subtle at first. He didn't like the way she laughed, calling it "cheesy" and embarrassing.

"Maya, why do you laugh like that in public?" Vivhaan said one evening as they drove home from a dinner party.

"What do you mean?" she asked, confused.

"It's just... loud. You draw attention to yourself. It's cheap," he said, his voice dripping with disdain.

Her smile faded, the joy of the evening snuffed out. That night, she lay awake, questioning if she had embarrassed him, if something was wrong with her. It was the beginning of a long, insidious erosion of her confidence.

Then it was her smile. "It's too cheap," he'd said one night, watching her as she posed for a photo with friends. Slowly, she stopped smiling. She stopped laughing. She stopped saying what was on her mind because every time she spoke, he'd twist her words, making her feel like she didn't know anything.

One evening, they had gone to a friend's party together. Maya, dressed in her favorite outfit, had been glowing. She chatted with friends and laughed freely for the first time in weeks. But as soon as they got into the car to leave, his mood shifted.

"You were really full of yourself tonight," he said, his words laced with venom.

"What? I was just having fun," she replied, taken aback.

"Fun? You were throwing yourself at everyone. Do you think I didn't notice the way you were laughing with Rahul?" he accused.

"Rahul? He's married! I wasn't—" she started, but he cut her off.

"You think I don't see what you're trying to do?" he said, his voice rising. "You make me look like an idiot."

Maya stared out the window, the weight of his words settling in her chest. That night, she cried herself to sleep, wondering if she had done something wrong.

*****

The First Slap

The first time Vivhaan hit her, it was as if the air had been sucked out of the room. They were arguing—again. Maya couldn't even remember what had sparked the fight, but it had escalated quickly. His temper was like a storm, sudden and violent.

"You don't respect me," he yelled, slamming his fist on the table.

"I'm trying, Vivhaan! But you're not even listening to me," Maya said, her voice trembling.

"Don't you dare raise your voice at me," he said, stepping closer, his face inches from hers.

"I'm not—" Before she could finish, his hand came down hard across her face. The slap echoed through the apartment, leaving her stunned. She stumbled back, her cheek stinging, her eyes welling up with tears.

He froze, his expression shifting from rage to panic. "I didn't mean to," he whispered, reaching for her. "You just... you made me so angry."

Maya backed away, her hand on her cheek. "You hit me," she said, her voice barely audible.

"I'm sorry," he said, his voice cracking. "It won't happen again. I promise."

But it did.

*****

The "Paternity Test" Incident

One memory that stood out like a scar was the day Maya casually mentioned she had missed her period for two weeks. They had been on the phone, and she brought it up with a nervous laugh. "Maybe I'm pregnant," she joked lightly, unsure of how he'd respond.

To her relief, he laughed it off too, making a joke about becoming a dad before they said goodnight. But the peace was short-lived. At 5 a.m., her phone rang, jolting her awake. It was Vivhaan, screaming on the other end.

"What the hell is this, Maya?!" he shouted.

"What are you talking about?" she asked groggily.

"You think you can trap me with a baby?" he accused, his voice full of venom. "I've already called my lawyer. We're getting a paternity test."

Maya sat up in bed, her heart pounding. "What? Vivhaan, I was joking. I'm not even—"

"Don't lie to me!" he interrupted. "My mother was right about you. You're nothing but a manipulative—"

She hung up, her hands trembling. Moments later, his mother called, her voice cold and accusatory. "You need to prove yourself," she said. "We can't take your word for it."

Maya sat on her bed, stunned, tears streaming down her face. She had no idea how things had escalated so quickly. Just hours ago, they had been laughing. Now, he was treating her like a liar, like someone who couldn't be trusted.

*****

The Birthday That Broke Her

Maya had always loved her birthday. It was the one day of the year when she felt truly celebrated. But her birthday with Vivhaan was different.

That evening, he had started drinking early, claiming it was to "loosen up" for the party. By the time the guests arrived, he was already slurring his words. Maya tried to cover for him, laughing off his inappropriate comments and steering conversations away from his drunken ramblings.

"Your friends don't even like me," he said later that night, after the guests had left.

"That's not true," Maya said, trying to soothe him.

"Don't lie to me," he snapped. "I saw the way they were looking at me. You've turned them against me."

The argument lasted for hours, with Vivhaan accusing her of being disloyal, ungrateful, and manipulative. By the end of the night, Maya was in tears, her birthday ruined.

The Wedding That Wasn't Hers

Another moment that lingered painfully in her mind was her brother's wedding. Maya had been over the moon with excitement. Her brother had finally found the love of his life, and the wedding was a celebration she had been looking forward to for months. Vivhaan had insisted on coming along, promising to be supportive. He was trying to get sober at the time, and Maya believed the trip might be good for him—a chance to see love in its purest form.

But instead of being a joyful occasion, the trip became a nightmare. Vivhaan found fault in everything. He complained about the time they spent at the venue, accusing her of ignoring him. He criticized her excitement, saying she was "acting like a child." The weekend, which should have been filled with happiness, turned into a string of fights and tension. It was during one of those arguments that the truth hit her like a ton of bricks: It's not the alcohol. It's him.

The realization was both liberating and devastating. For so long, she had blamed his drinking, telling herself that things would get better once he stopped. But now she understood that his controlling, manipulative behavior was a part of him—alcohol or not.

The weeks after the wedding were tense. Maya found herself pushing back against his control for the first time, speaking up in ways she hadn't before. But every time she did, he turned it against her, saying she was becoming "too argumentative" or "too aggressive." The more she reclaimed her voice, the louder their fights became.

One evening, after yet another argument, Vivhaan dropped a bombshell: "My friends don't trust you. They think I should leave you."

Maya stared at him, her chest tightening. She realized this wasn't just about his friends. It was about control. He was trying to scare her into submission, to make her feel small and unworthy. But this time, she didn't shrink. "If that's what you want, leave," she said firmly. Her voice didn't shake. She was done playing his games.

His reaction was explosive. The argument escalated, and in the heat of the moment, he slapped her again. Maya froze, her cheek stinging from the blow. She stared at him, the man she had once loved so deeply, and realized he wasn't the man she thought he was.

But stupid, silly love pulled her back in. She forgave him, hoping—praying—that this time, things would change. They didn't.

*****

The Final Straw

The day before Vivhaan left for rehab, everything truly fell apart. They had been arguing again, their voices echoing through the apartment. And then, in a moment of blind rage, he grabbed her by the neck and choked her.

Maya clawed at his hands, gasping for air, her vision blurring as the seconds ticked by. And then, just as suddenly as it started, he let go. She collapsed to the floor, coughing and trembling. He stood over her, his face a mask of guilt and panic. "I'm sorry," he whispered, but she wasn't listening anymore.

When she finally regained her strength, she stood, grabbed her bag, and walked out the door. He begged her to stay, to forgive him, but this time, she didn't turn back.

*****

Vivhaan went to rehab the next day, and for the first time in years, Maya felt like she could breathe. Her laughter returned. Her smile came back. She started speaking her mind again, no longer afraid of being silenced or judged. But even as she rediscovered herself, Vivhaan lingered in her thoughts. The good, the bad, the ugly—it all came flooding back, haunting her in quiet moments. She wasn't sure if she would ever be free of him completely. But she was sure of one thing: she would never go back.

The Return of Vivhaan—And the Ghosts of Their Past

Two weeks to Vivhaan's return. Maya had spent that time rediscovering herself, immersing herself in the small but meaningful parts of life that she had abandoned during their tumultuous relationship. She'd reconnected with her friends, her passions, and even with her own body—something she had neglected while she was constantly giving her energy to someone who never truly appreciated it.

But now, Vivhaan was coming back. She hadn't been sure what she expected. Part of her had braced herself for the inevitable moment when he would try to worm his way back into her life, his familiar voice sweet-talking its way through the cracks in her resolve. But the part of her that had healed, that had learned to love herself again, was ready. Or at least, she hoped she was.

She sat on her bed, absently flipping through a book she had recently picked up, but her mind was miles away. Every so often, her gaze drifted to her phone, waiting for a text, an email, a call—any sign that Vivhaan was trying to re-enter her life. But when the phone did finally buzz, it wasn't Vivhaan. It was Tara.

"Heard anything from Vivhaan yet? You okay?" Tara's message read. Maya exhaled a deep breath before typing back, her fingers hesitating over the keys for a moment.

"He's coming back soon. I don't know how I feel about it."

"You've come so far, Maya. Don't let him take you back to where you were."

Maya smiled at the reminder. She had come far, hadn't she? It felt almost surreal—her life without Vivhaan. For so long, he had been her center, the axis on which everything in her world had turned. And now, she was her own center. She had taken control back, but was she really ready for what was coming?

*****

The day Vivhaan returned, the air felt heavy. Maya tried to keep herself busy, running errands and tidying her apartment, but nothing could stop the steady drumbeat of anxiety in her chest. Around noon, her phone buzzed again. This time, it was him.

"Can I see you today?" the text read.

Her heart stuttered. For a moment, she considered ignoring it, but she knew she couldn't. Running from him wasn't the answer—not anymore. She needed to face him, to prove to herself that she was stronger now.

"Fine. Meet me at the café on Main Street. 4 PM," she replied.

The hours leading up to the meeting felt endless. She rehearsed what she wanted to say, reminding herself of all the reasons she had left. But when she walked into the café and saw him sitting there, everything she'd prepared seemed to vanish.

Vivhaan looked... different. There was a fragility about him, a vulnerability she hadn't seen before. His eyes lit up when he saw her, and for a moment, she hated how her heart betrayed her with a pang of longing.

"Maya," he said, standing as she approached the table.

"Vivhaan," she replied, keeping her tone steady.

They sat down, and for a moment, neither of them spoke. The silence stretched between them like a chasm, filled with everything they couldn't say.

"You look good," he finally said, his voice soft.

"Thanks," she replied curtly. "You wanted to talk?"

He nodded, running a hand through his hair. "I've been in therapy. Rehab, too. I've been trying to fix myself, Maya. I know I hurt you. I know I ruined everything."

She folded her arms, leaning back in her chair. "And what do you want from me? Forgiveness? Closure? Or do you want me to forget everything and pretend it never happened?"

"No," he said quickly. "I don't expect you to forget. I just... I needed to see you. To tell you that I'm sorry. I've changed."

"Changed?" she said, her voice rising slightly. "Vivhaan, do you even understand what you put me through? The nights I cried myself to sleep? The constant fear of what mood you'd be in? The way you made me question my own worth?"

His face crumpled, and for a moment, she saw the pain in his eyes. But it wasn't enough. Not for her. Not anymore.

"I was broken," he said. "I didn't know how to love you the way you deserved. But I'm trying now. Please, Maya, give me a chance to prove it."

She shook her head, tears welling up in her eyes. "It's easy to say you've changed when I'm not there to see it. It's easy to promise the world when you're sitting across a table. But Vivhaan, do you know how hard it is to rebuild yourself after someone has torn you apart? I can't go back. I won't."

He reached across the table, his hand hovering over hers. "I love you, Maya. I always have."

She pulled her hand away, her voice trembling but firm. "Loving me didn't stop you from hurting me. Loving me didn't stop you from breaking me. And now, I've finally learned to love myself enough to say no."

Vivhaan leaned back, his shoulders slumping. "So this is it?"

"This is it," she said, her voice steady despite the tears streaming down her face. "I hope you find peace, Vivhaan. I really do. But I can't be a part of your journey anymore."

She stood, grabbing her bag and walking away without looking back. Each step felt like a victory, a reminder of how far she had come. And as she stepped out into the sunlight, she felt a weight lift from her shoulders.

The Echo of the Past

Maya sat on her balcony, the evening breeze teasing her hair, carrying the faint sounds of traffic and distant laughter. The city lights blinked at her like tiny stars scattered across the urban sprawl, but tonight, they brought no comfort. Her thoughts weren't with the shimmering view; they were with Vivhaan.

She closed her eyes and let out a shaky breath. "Why now?" she whispered to no one in particular. It had been months since she left, but the memories were persistent, clinging to her like shadows she couldn't shake.

The chair beneath her creaked as she shifted, pulling her knees up to her chest. She stared at her phone lying on the table next to her, the screen dark. It had been silent for hours, yet the mere presence of it felt oppressive. What if he reached out again? What if he didn't? Both thoughts unsettled her in equal measure.

"Was it all a lie?" she muttered, her voice breaking slightly.

The good moments—they had felt so real. The way he'd held her hand when she was nervous, the quiet nights they'd spent watching old movies, the way he'd told her she was the best thing that had ever happened to him. Were those moments just illusions? Or had they been real, twisted into something unrecognizable by his demons?

Her mind, traitorous as always, drifted back to the first time she saw him drunk. The memory played out like a film she couldn't stop.

*****

"You're not listening to me!" Vivhaan's voice was loud, slurred. He stumbled slightly as he waved the half-empty bottle in his hand. They had just returned from a party, and Maya had barely gotten her shoes off before the argument began.

"I'm listening, Vivhaan," she said softly, trying to keep her voice calm, steady. "But you're drunk. Let's talk about this tomorrow, okay?"

"No!" he snapped, his eyes narrowing. "You always do this. You always think you're so much better than me, don't you?"

"Vivhaan, stop," she whispered, her heart pounding. She had never seen him like this before—so unhinged, so cruel.

But he didn't stop. "You're just like everyone else," he spat. "You'll leave me the second things get hard. You're a coward, Maya."

The words hit her like a slap. She wanted to yell back, to defend herself, but all she could do was stare at him, her throat tight with unshed tears.

*****

Maya opened her eyes, blinking away the sting of the memory. Her chest felt heavy, like there was a weight pressing down on her.

She picked up her phone, scrolling absently through her messages until she found Tara's name. Her thumb hovered over the screen for a moment before she started typing.

"I hate this," she wrote. "I feel like I've moved on, but then nights like this happen, and it all comes back."

The reply came almost immediately.

"You're allowed to feel that way, Maya. Healing isn't linear. But don't forget how far you've come. Don't let him pull you back into that darkness."

Maya sighed, her fingers tightening around the phone. "What if I made a mistake? What if leaving wasn't the right choice?"

Tara's response took a little longer this time, and when it came, it was direct, almost harsh.

"You didn't make a mistake. You chose yourself, Maya. You chose your peace. Don't second-guess that just because you're feeling lonely tonight."

Maya placed the phone back on the table, her stomach twisting with guilt and uncertainty. Tara was right. She knew Tara was right. But that didn't make the ache in her chest any less real.

Her hands trembled slightly as she poured herself a cup of tea, the warmth of the mug grounding her. But her mind was still restless, still circling back to the same question:

"What if?"

What if she had tried harder? What if she had been more patient, more understanding? What if she had stayed?

She shook her head, muttering to herself. "Stop it. Stop romanticizing it. You know how it ends."

But the doubts were louder tonight. The silence of her apartment, usually so comforting, felt suffocating. She imagined his voice, the way he used to call her name like it was a secret only they shared. She imagined his laugh, his touch. For a fleeting moment, she almost missed him.

Almost.

*****

The sound of her phone buzzing pulled her back to reality. Her heart jumped as she glanced at the screen. For a moment, she thought it might be him.

But it wasn't. It was Tara again.

"Don't let the past win. You're stronger than this, Maya. You're stronger than him."

A tear slid down Maya's cheek as she read the message. She wiped it away quickly, taking a deep breath.

"Tara's right," she whispered. "I am stronger than this."

She set the mug down and stood, walking back to the balcony. The city stretched out before her, vast and unending. It reminded her that there was a world beyond Vivhaan, beyond the pain he had caused.

She closed her eyes, letting the cool air wash over her. And for the first time that night, she allowed herself to feel proud.

Proud of the decision she had made, proud of the person she was becoming.

"Goodbye, Vivhaan," she said softly, her voice steady despite the tears still streaming down her face. "You're not my burden to carry anymore."

The words felt final, like the closing of a door she had left ajar for far too long.

And as she stood there, the city lights flickering in the distance, Maya realized something she hadn't before.

She was free.

And that was enough.

The Other Side of the Story

Maya's words echoed in Vivhaan's mind long after she had walked out the door. *"You don't deserve me. You don't even see me."* He had replayed that moment a thousand times, each time feeling the weight of her absence grow heavier.

Now, sitting in his darkened room, the curtains drawn tight, the air thick with the stale scent of whiskey and regret, Vivhaan felt the full force of his failure. The empty bottle on the nightstand taunted him, the dim glow of his phone casting shadows across the walls. His mind buzzed with restless energy, thoughts clashing and colliding, each more unbearable than the last

He thought back to his childhood, to the nights he had spent hiding in his room while his parents screamed at each other downstairs. He had learned early on that love was something fragile, something that could shatter at any moment. And yet, he had clung to Maya, desperate to prove that he could be different, that he could be the man she deserved. But now, as he sat there alone, he realized that he had become everything he had once feared.

The rehab counselors had told him sobriety would bring clarity, but all it brought was noise. Deafening, unrelenting noise. He reached for his phone, scrolling aimlessly, hoping to find a distraction. There were no new messages, no missed calls. Nothing. Just silence.

He stared at the bottle again. "You're gone, but the damage's already done, isn't it?" he muttered bitterly, his voice scratchy from the lack of sleep.

Maya. Her name hung in the room like a phantom, refusing to leave him alone. He squeezed his eyes shut, trying to drown out the image of her face, the sound of her voice, but it was no use. She was everywhere.

"Did I really lose her?" he asked aloud, his tone somewhere between anger and desperation.

The answer was obvious, but he couldn't bring himself to say it. He had told himself so many times that Maya leaving was her fault, not his. She hadn't been patient enough, hadn't understood what he was going through. She had abandoned him when he needed her the most.

But another voice—a quieter, sharper one—whispered the truth he couldn't escape. *You pushed her away. You chose the bottle over her every single time.*

Vivhaan slammed his fist against the table, the sharp pain grounding him for a moment. "No," he hissed through gritted teeth. "She could've stayed. She could've fought harder."

The night she left replayed in his mind, a relentless loop that refused to fade.

He had been drunk, of course. The argument was blurry, but he remembered the rage—the way it had bubbled up inside him, uncontrollable, vicious.

"You're always running!" he had shouted, his words slurring together. "Every time things get hard, you just... you leave!"

"I'm not running, Vivhaan. I'm done," Maya had said, her voice shaking but firm. "I can't do this anymore."

Her words had hit him like a punch to the gut, but instead of showing her his pain, he lashed out. "Fine, leave! That's all you're good at anyway. You think you're perfect? You're not. You're just as broken as I am, but at least I admit it!"

He didn't even remember how she responded. He only remembered the sound of the door closing behind her.

*****

Vivhaan rubbed his temples, his anger simmering just below the surface. Why couldn't she have stayed? Why couldn't she have understood how hard it was for him?

"She didn't care enough," he whispered, his voice cracking. But even as the words left his mouth, they felt hollow.

The truth—no matter how much he tried to ignore it—was that Maya had cared. She had cared more than anyone else ever had. And he had destroyed that.

"Damn it!" he shouted, grabbing the empty bottle and hurling it across the room. It shattered against the wall, pieces scattering across the floor. The sound echoed in the silence, a violent reminder of his own destruction.

He sat back, breathing heavily, his hands shaking. He hated himself in that moment. But more than that, he hated her for leaving.

*****

In the suffocating silence, his thoughts turned darker, angrier. The rehab counselors had fed him lines about accountability and self-forgiveness, but what did they know? They didn't understand what it was like to be him, to carry the weight of his own failures every single day.

"She wanted too much from me," he muttered, his voice defensive. "No one could live up to her expectations. She wanted me to be perfect, to have all the answers. That's not fair."

But the quieter voice—the one he kept trying to silence—spoke again. *She didn't want perfect. She wanted you to try. And you didn't.*

Vivhaan clenched his fists, his nails digging into his palms. He didn't want to hear that voice anymore. He didn't want to admit that he had failed her, that he had failed himself. It was easier to stay angry, to blame her for walking away, than to face the truth.

"She gave up," he said, louder this time, as if saying it with more conviction would make it real. "She didn't even give me a chance."

But deep down, he knew that wasn't true. Maya had given him more chances than he deserved. She had stayed through the lies, the manipulation, the broken promises. She had stayed until she couldn't anymore.

And now, she was gone.

*****

Vivhaan got up and paced the room, his anger bubbling over into frustration. He kicked a chair, sending it toppling over, then ran his hands through his hair, pulling at it as if he could yank the guilt out of his skull.

"She didn't have to leave," he said again, his voice hoarse. "She could've stayed. She could've helped me."

But even as he said it, he knew it wasn't her responsibility. It had never been her job to fix him. That was the part that made him angriest—not at her, but at himself. Because deep down, he knew he had ruined the one good thing in his life.

But he wasn't ready to admit that yet. He wasn't ready to let go of the anger, the blame, the denial.

Because if he did, what was left? Just him. Just the broken pieces of a man who didn't know how to put himself back together.

Vivhaan sank onto the bed, his head in his hands. The tears came then, hot and uncontrollable, but he didn't fight them. They were the only release he had left.

In the darkness of his room, with the shards of the broken bottle glinting faintly on the floor, Vivhaan allowed himself to cry. But even in his grief, he couldn't bring himself to say the words that haunted him most.

I lost her because of me.

Instead, he whispered into the silence, his voice trembling with anger and sorrow. "She should've stayed."

And with that, the room fell silent once more, leaving him alone with his guilt, his rage, and the unbearable weight of everything he refused to accept.

A Journey Back to Maya's Self

Maya sat cross-legged on her bed, her journal open on her lap, the pen poised but unmoving. The soft hum of the city outside her window filled the room, a constant reminder that life was moving forward. She was supposed to be writing about gratitude—her therapist's latest assignment—but her mind wandered, as it so often did, back to Vivhaan.

She missed him.

The thought crept in uninvited, unwelcome, but undeniable. Not the drunken fights, not the screaming matches, not the nights she spent crying herself to sleep. But she missed *him*. The way he'd hold her hand in the car and absentmindedly trace circles on her palm. The way his laugh filled the room, boyish and carefree, in the rare moments when he wasn't carrying the weight of his own demons.

Maya let the pen fall onto the page as she sighed deeply.

It wasn't fair how memory worked, was it? How her brain seemed to latch onto the good moments as if they could outweigh the unbearable ones. How her heart seemed to ache for the version of Vivhaan who only existed in fleeting moments, not the man who had so often left her feeling like she was gasping for air.

"Why do I do this to myself?" she whispered aloud, the sound of her voice breaking the stillness.

Her phone buzzed on the nightstand, and for a brief, irrational second, she thought it might be him. It wasn't. Just a message from her friend Tara:

"How's my strong, independent queen doing?"

Maya smiled faintly, but the weight in her chest didn't lift. She typed back a quick reply.

"I'm okay. Just thinking too much, as usual."

Tara responded almost immediately.

"You've got this. Remember how far you've come. Missing him doesn't mean you're weak—it means you're human."

Maya placed the phone face down, her thoughts spiraling.

She had come so far, hadn't she? The woman she was now wouldn't tolerate what she had endured back then. The gaslighting. The manipulation. The endless cycle of apologies and broken promises. But it didn't mean she didn't miss the comfort of having someone. The feeling of belonging to someone.

"Stop romanticizing it," she told herself sternly, but her own voice didn't sound convincing.

Her mind flitted back to the night they danced in her living room, barefoot, the world outside forgotten. He'd spun her around, his grin infectious, and for a brief moment, it had felt like a fairytale. She had been *happy* then, hadn't she?

But happiness and love weren't the same thing, she reminded herself. And whatever that fleeting happiness was, it had come at a cost—her peace.

Maya stood and wandered to the window, staring out at the city lights. She wrapped her arms around herself, the cool glass against her forehead. How could she feel so strong and so fragile at the same time? How could she finally be free, yet still yearn for the pieces of a man who had broken her?

Because for all the horrible moments, there were good ones too. There were stolen kisses on rainy nights, whispered secrets in the dark, the way he would look at her as if she were the only thing in the world that mattered. And she had loved him for that, loved him in ways that scared her, because she had handed over pieces of herself she could never get back.

She closed her eyes, letting the tears come, the ache of missing him washing over her like a tidal wave.

"I don't miss *him*," she whispered, her voice shaky. "I miss the way I felt when it was good."

But it wasn't always good.

Maya clenched her jaw, trying to remind herself of the nights she had lain awake, terrified of his mood swings, of the cruel words he'd throw at her without warning. The nights when she begged him to stop drinking, only to be met with hollow promises and dismissive shrugs. She didn't deserve that. She never had.

Her phone buzzed again, and this time she ignored it. She didn't need validation right now. She needed honesty—from herself.

"Maybe that's the hardest part," she murmured. "Letting go of the good along with the bad."

Because as much as she wanted to hate him, as much as she needed to keep her distance, there would always be a part of her that wished he could have been the man she thought he was in the beginning. The man she had fallen for.

But he wasn't.

And no amount of wishing could change that.

Maya wiped her tears and stepped back from the window. She sat down at her desk, pulling her journal closer. This time, the words came easily, pouring out of her like a confession:

**"I miss the illusion of us. The dream of what we could have been. But I don't miss the nights I cried myself to sleep. I don't miss walking on eggshells. I don't miss losing myself in the name of love.

I can miss him and still know I'm better off without him. I can grieve the good moments and still choose myself."**

She put the pen down and took a deep breath. The ache was still there, but it was lighter now, less suffocating.

Maya wasn't done healing. She knew that. But she also knew that missing him didn't mean she had made the wrong choice. It just meant she was human. And that was okay.

Vivhaan's Struggle for Control

The meeting had gone better than she had hoped. Maya was practically glowing as she walked back to her desk, her laptop tucked under her arm and a coffee cup in hand. Her team had nailed the pitch, and their client was thrilled. For once, everything seemed to be falling into place, and the weight of the past few months felt lighter.

As she reached her desk, her colleague and friend, Naina, looked up from her screen. "Maya, that dress looks so good on you. I love the color—it makes you glow!"

Maya paused, caught off guard but pleasantly surprised by the compliment. "Oh, thanks, Naina! I wasn't sure about it when I bought it, but I guess it's growing on me."

Naina smiled warmly. "No, seriously. Wear more colors like that—you're rocking it!"

Maya nodded with a small laugh, but as she sat down, Naina's words triggered an unwelcome memory. Her smile faltered for just a moment as her mind wandered to a time she had tried to "dress up" for someone else's approval.

*****

It was one of those strained Sunday brunches with Vivhaan's mother—an occasion Maya never looked forward to. She had opted for a simple white kurta with delicate embroidery, pairing it with silver earrings. She had felt comfortable, but the second she walked through the door, she knew it wouldn't be enough.

"Ah, Maya," Vivhaan's mother had said, her sharp eyes scanning her from head to toe. "You really should consider dressing up a bit more when you visit us. Presentation is important, dear. How else will you ever fit in?"

Maya froze, her fingers tightening around the gift bag she had brought. "What's wrong with what I'm wearing?" she asked, keeping her tone polite but firm.

Vivhaan's mother let out a light, condescending laugh. "It's just... plain, isn't it? A little effort wouldn't hurt. Maybe something brighter, more elegant. You're a pretty girl—you should show it."

Maya clenched her jaw, feeling the heat rise to her cheeks. Before she could respond, Vivhaan walked into the room, oblivious to the tension. "What's going on?" he asked, glancing between the two women.

"Nothing, dear," his mother said sweetly, then turned back to Maya. "I'm just offering some advice. I know it can be hard to hear, but it's for your own good."

"Advice?" Maya snapped, unable to hold back. "You mean telling me I'm not good enough the way I am?"

The smile vanished from his mother's face. "Don't be rude, Maya. I'm just trying to help."

Vivhaan's brows furrowed as he stepped closer. "Maya, can you not—"

"No, Vivhaan," Maya interrupted, her voice trembling with anger. "This isn't the first time she's said something like this. And every time, you just stand there and let it happen."

"Okay, enough," Vivhaan said, raising his voice. "Can we not do this right now?"

Maya stared at him, incredulous. "Right now? When, Vivhaan? When it's convenient for you? Maybe if you actually stood up for me for once, we wouldn't *have* to do this."

"Don't drag me into your insecurities," he shot back, his tone cold.

Maya felt the sting of his words, her eyes welling up despite her best efforts. She turned on her heel and walked out of the room, ignoring his mother's smug expression as she left.

*****

Maya blinked, shaking her head as she came back to the present. The weight of that memory sat heavy in her chest, but it didn't linger like it used to. She looked down at her dress—a deep teal that brought out the warmth in her skin. She had chosen it for herself, not for anyone else's approval.

Naina's compliment floated back to her, pulling her out of the dark spiral. She smiled softly, turning her chair toward her friend. "Thanks again, Naina. I needed that."

Her friend looked up, confused but happy. "For what?"

"For reminding me that I'm doing just fine on my own," Maya said with a wink, her voice light but firm.

As the smile spread across her face, she felt a quiet sense of relief and power. She wasn't that version of herself anymore—the one who needed validation from people who would never give it. She had chosen herself, and for the first time in a long time, that felt like enough.

*****

That afternoon, Maya sat across from Raj at their favorite Italian café, the smell of freshly baked bread and simmering tomato sauce wafting through the air. The place buzzed with the usual lunchtime crowd, and for the first time in weeks, Maya felt a little lighter.

"Okay, okay, but seriously," Raj said, gesturing animatedly with his fork. "You should have seen her face when I told her the budget was non-negotiable. Priceless."

Maya chuckled, twirling her pasta. "You really do have a way with words, don't you?"

"Of course. It's a gift," Raj replied with a mock bow, making her laugh even harder.

For a moment, everything felt normal—easy. But then Raj leaned back in his chair, giving her an appraising look. "By the way, that dress suits you, Maya. You look great."

She smiled, about to thank him, but the words caught in her throat. His compliment, so genuine and kind, triggered a memory she had tried to bury.

It was late one evening, months ago. Maya had just returned home after dinner with Raj—a perfectly platonic meal that had left her feeling refreshed after a long week. But the second she walked through the door, she knew something was wrong.

Vivhaan was sitting on the couch, a glass of whiskey in his hand, his eyes glassy and sharp.

"How was your little date?" he asked, his voice low but simmering with anger.

Maya froze, taken aback. "What? It wasn't a date, Vivhaan. I told you, Raj and I—"

"Oh, spare me," he snapped, standing up and pacing the room. "You think I don't see how you look at him? Or how he looks at you?"

She shook her head, frustration bubbling up. "Raj is my friend, Vivhaan. That's it. You know that."

"Do I?" he challenged, turning to face her. His tone grew colder, more venomous. "He's better than me, isn't he? That's what you're thinking. He's successful, charming, perfect—everything I'm not."

"That's not true!" Maya protested, her voice trembling.

"Don't lie to me!" he roared, the glass in his hand trembling as he gestured wildly. "You'd rather be with him. Admit it! Why wouldn't you? He's so much better than me, right?"

Tears welled up in her eyes as she struggled to stay calm. "Vivhaan, please. This isn't about Raj. This is about you and me. Why can't you see that?"

But he didn't hear her. Or maybe he didn't want to. He downed the rest of his drink, his jaw tight with fury. "If you want him, just go," he muttered bitterly. "I won't stop you."

The words stung, and for a moment, she couldn't breathe. "That's not fair," she whispered. "You're drunk, and you're angry, and you're taking it out on me."

He let out a bitter laugh, setting his glass down with a sharp clink. "Maybe I am. But you don't get to play innocent, Maya. Not when you're the one who keeps running to him."

The argument spiraled from there, his words growing harsher, cutting deeper. She tried to reason with him, to make him see the truth, but it was like shouting into a storm. By the time she finally retreated to the bedroom, her heart felt like it had been ripped in two.

*****

"Earth to Maya," Raj's voice broke through her thoughts, pulling her back to the present.

She blinked, realizing she had been staring at her plate, her fork poised mid-air. "Sorry," she said quickly, forcing a smile. "Got lost in my head for a second."

Raj raised an eyebrow, his expression softening. "You okay? You looked like you were a million miles away."

"I'm fine," she assured him, setting her fork down. "Just... thinking about how much better this lasagna is than anything I've had in a while."

He chuckled, but there was a trace of concern in his eyes. "Well, if there's anything else you're chewing on, you know I'm here, right?"

She nodded, grateful for his kindness. "I know. Thanks, Raj."

As the conversation shifted back to lighter topics, Maya felt a small wave of relief wash over her. She wasn't in that place anymore. The Maya who had been silenced by Vivhaan's anger, who had questioned her own worth in the face of his insecurities—that wasn't her anymore.

She glanced at Raj, his easy smile and genuine laughter filling the space between them. For the first time in a long time, she felt at peace, knowing she had made the right choice to walk away.

*****

While Maya was moving on, somewhere Vivhaan was playing the memory of the night before he left rehab, Vivhaan lay in bed, staring up at the ceiling, his mind racing. He knew the road ahead wouldn't be smooth. It wouldn't be easy to win back Maya's trust, if that was even possible. But he was willing to try. He had to.

His thoughts were interrupted by the sound of the door opening. One of the counselors entered, her presence calm and reassuring.

"You ready for tomorrow?" she asked softly.

Vivhaan nodded, forcing a small smile. "I think so."

As he prepared to leave, the weight of the past few months settled heavily on his chest. But as he packed his things, he realized that he wasn't the same person who had entered rehab. He wasn't cured. His demons still lurked in the shadows, but he had learned to confront them. He had learned that healing was a lifelong process, not a quick fix.

And as for Maya—he didn't know if she would ever forgive him, if she would ever let him back into her life. But he was determined to try. For her. For himself. And for the future that he had almost lost.

*****

Vivhaan took a deep breath as he stepped outside, the fresh air of freedom hitting him like a wave. There was a long road ahead, but he was ready to walk it. He was ready to face whatever came next, and maybe, just maybe, he would be able to prove that he could be the man Maya deserved.

Vivhaan's Return

"You think you're perfect? You're nothing without me!" he had shouted, the words hitting her like blows. She had stood there, silent, tears streaming down her face, too stunned to respond. In that moment, something inside her had broken. She had believed him. She had let his words seep into her soul, convincing herself that she wasn't enough.

Now, in the quiet of her apartment, Maya clenched her fists, her nails digging into her palms. She hated that those memories still had power over her, that they still made her question herself. But she reminded herself of the truth: She had survived. She had rebuilt her life piece by piece, and she was stronger now than she had ever been.

Vivhaan, meanwhile, couldn't let go. His desperation was palpable, and his persistence relentless. He sent text after text, each one a variation of the same plea: "I miss you." "I'm sorry." "Please, Maya."

Her resolve wavered at times. Not because she wanted him back, but because she was tired—tired of carrying the weight of their past, tired of the guilt that whispered she was being too harsh. She replayed their last conversation in her mind, hearing his voice crack as he said, "I just want to make things right." For a moment, she had almost believed him.

But then she remembered the nights she had cried herself to sleep, the fear that had gripped her every time he lost his temper, the suffocating weight of his control. She had promised herself she would never go back to that, no matter how much he claimed to have changed.

One night, her phone buzzed with another text. She didn't even have to look to know it was him. She let it sit there, unread, as she turned off her phone and crawled into bed. She stared at the ceiling, her mind racing with memories—good ones, bad ones, and everything in between. She remembered the way he used to make her laugh, the way he had held her when she cried. But those moments felt like a lifetime ago, like they had belonged to a different version of herself.

The version of herself who had believed in him, who had fought for him, was gone. She wasn't the same woman who had clung to the hope that he would change. She was Maya—whole, independent, strong. And she wasn't going to let him drag her back into the darkness.

The next morning, Maya woke to a clear blue sky and a sense of clarity she hadn't felt in years. She knew Vivhaan would keep trying, but she also knew she didn't owe him anything. Not her time, not her forgiveness, and certainly not her heart.

Vivhaan, on the other hand, stood outside her building later that day, a bouquet of flowers in hand and hope in his eyes. He had spent hours choosing them—roses, her favorite, mixed with daisies because she'd once told him they made her smile. He remembered how much she used to love flowers, how her face would light up when she received them. But Maya didn't come down. She didn't answer his texts or his calls. She had already made her decision, and no amount of grand gestures would change that.

As he stood there, clutching the bouquet, a bitter memory surfaced—one he had tried to bury. It was her birthday, or maybe it was some other special occasion; he couldn't remember now. She had mentioned, almost shyly, how much she loved flowers. "They make everything feel brighter," she'd said, her voice light, hopeful. But instead of listening, he had brushed her off with a dismissive laugh. *"Flowers? Really? What a waste of money. They just die in a few days anyway."* The way her smile had faltered, the way her eyes had dimmed—it haunted him now. He hadn't just ignored her; he'd been cruel.

And now, here he was, standing outside her building with the very thing she had once told him would make her happy. It meant nothing now. The flowers were a hollow gesture, a desperate attempt to patch a wound he had inflicted long ago. He realized, in that moment, that it wasn't just Maya who had changed—it was him too. But no bouquet could undo the damage, no flowers could erase the pain.

He turned away from her building, the bouquet still clutched in his hand, and felt the weight of his own failures settle over him. This wasn't just about her not coming down. It was about the realization that he had waited too long to care, too long to change, and now, there was no going back.

Later that night, his text came through again: "I miss you. I'm sorry."

This time, she didn't hesitate. She deleted the message, her fingers steady, her heart light. For the first time in a long time, Maya felt truly free.

The Weight of the Past

Even though Maya had walked away, even though she was carving out a new life for herself, Vivhaan's shadow lingered. Each morning, as she sipped her coffee on the tiny balcony of her new apartment, she felt the weight of his absence and presence simultaneously. Her days were becoming lighter—she had started taking pottery classes at a studio nearby, her fingers finding solace in the malleable clay. Yet, there were moments, like when she heard a certain song or caught a fleeting scent of his cologne in the air, that pulled her back into the memories she was trying to escape. Maya fought through these moments, leaning on her newfound routines—morning runs in the park, late-night journaling sessions—to remind herself that she was more than the pain he had left behind. His presence, no matter how distant, still haunted her thoughts, a reminder of what she had left behind. But while Maya was beginning to embrace her freedom, Vivhaan's world was unraveling in a way she couldn't have imagined. The distance between them was growing, but so was the weight of his actions.

Vivhaan stared out the window of his room, the midday sun casting a pale glow on his face. His body was exhausted from the months of withdrawal, but his mind was restless. He hadn't been sober for long enough to fully grasp the reality of what had happened between him and Maya, but every passing day felt like a heavy brick pressing down on his chest.

He knew he had been wrong. The gaslighting, the manipulation, the drinking—it was all so clear to him now, though he had never seen it like that before. He could still hear her voice trembling as she once asked him why he always made her question her own memories. He could see her tear-streaked face during one of their final arguments, the way her hands shook as she tried to defend her reality while he twisted it into something unrecognizable. These moments replayed in his mind like a haunting, each one driving home the depth of the pain he had caused. He had been blind to it, thinking that he could fix everything, that he could make her stay, that he could make her love him again. But in reality, he had destroyed the very thing that had once brought them together.

In the quiet hours of the night, as he lay on his back staring at the ceiling, Vivhaan's thoughts would return to Maya—her laugh, the way she made him feel like he was worth something. There had been moments, beautiful moments, when he had truly believed that they were building something real. But it hadn't been real. It was all just a facade, a version of love that he had crafted in his own mind, one that didn't allow for mistakes or vulnerability, one that was poisoned by his own insecurities and need for control.

He remembered the last time he had seen Maya, how desperate he had been to hold on to something that was slipping away. He had tried to make her feel guilty, tried to make her believe that she was the one in the wrong. But she hadn't taken the bait. Maya had stood her ground, her eyes filled with a quiet strength he had never truly seen before. It was that moment—when she finally walked away—that had broken him, in ways he hadn't yet fully understood.

But , Vivhaan was beginning to understand. He had begun attending group therapy sessions, listening to the stories of others who had been trapped in their own cycles of addiction and self-destruction. There were moments when he felt a glimmer of hope, a belief that maybe, just maybe, he could change. But those moments were fleeting, overshadowed by the weight of his guilt.

He had hurt Maya in ways that words couldn't express. And now, he had to live with that reality.

Maya had been his anchor, and in many ways, she still was. He could feel her influence in the smallest of things—like how he would instinctively reach for chamomile tea instead of his usual whiskey, a habit she had introduced him to when he struggled with insomnia. Even his newfound interest in journaling, something she swore by, carried her ghost. It was as though she had etched pieces of herself into his life, and now, in her absence, those pieces weighed heavily on him, reminding him of all he had lost. The memories of their time together haunted him, and though he had pushed her away, part of him still longed for the connection they had shared. But Vivhaan knew he couldn't just go back to her. He couldn't pick up the pieces and expect her to fit them back together. She had already moved on, and for the first time,

Vivhaan realized that he wasn't entitled to her love. He had lost that right the moment he had let his demons take control.

As he sat in the group therapy circle one afternoon, Vivhaan's hands fidgeted in his lap. The room was quiet, the only sound the faint hum of the air conditioner. When the counselor asked, "What are you willing to do to make things right?" the words sliced through the stillness, catching him off guard. He froze, his thoughts colliding in a chaotic tangle.

The question echoed in his mind, louder and louder, until it felt like the walls were closing in. For a moment, he saw Maya's face—her smile, the way she would tilt her head slightly when she was curious. Then, the darker memories rushed in: her tear-filled eyes during their fights, the way her voice trembled when she told him she couldn't do it anymore. A lump formed in his throat. What was he willing to do?

The memories clawed at him, unrelenting. Every false promise he had made, every lie he had told, resurfaced with brutal clarity. *"I'll stop drinking, I swear,"* he had told her once after she found him passed out on the couch, the smell of alcohol heavy in the air. She had believed him then, wiping away her tears and cradling his face as though her love alone could fix him. But by the next week, he was back to his old habits, convincing himself that she would forgive him. She always did.

He remembered the way he used her emotions to keep her tied to him, a cruel manipulation masked as vulnerability. He had weaponized her empathy, twisting her love into something he could exploit. Once, during one of their worst fights, she had threatened to leave. He had grabbed her wrist—

not forcefully, but enough to stop her in her tracks—and whispered, *"If you walk out that door, I don't know what I'll do to myself."* He had watched the fight drain out of her, her resolve crumbling under the weight of his words. She stayed that night, just like he knew she would. He had used her love against her, trapping her in a cycle of guilt and obligation.

Another memory surfaced—one that made his stomach churn with shame. They had been at dinner with her friends, a rare occasion when she tried to reconnect with the life she had before him. She had laughed at something one of them said, a genuine, unrestrained laugh that lit up the room. But instead of feeling happy for her, he had felt threatened. On the way home, he had lashed out. *"You seemed a little too happy with them,"* he had sneered. *"Maybe you should just stay with them next time."* The words had cut deep; he had seen it in her face. But she hadn't argued. She had just sat in silence, staring out the window, retreating further into herself.

And then there were the broken promises about therapy, about changing. *"I'll go next week,"* he had told her more times than he could count. But he never did. Each time she brought it up, he found a way to deflect, to make her feel like she was asking for too much. *"Why can't you just trust me?"* he had snapped during one argument, his voice dripping with indignation.

The weight of all these moments crashed down on him as he sat in that therapy circle. Everything she had once believed in—his love, his promises—he had shattered. She had given him her trust, her patience, her unwavering support, and he had turned it all to ash.

The counselor's voice broke through his spiraling thoughts. "Vivhaan, what do you need to confront to move forward?"

He hesitated, his voice barely above a whisper. "Everything," he admitted, his hands tightening into fists. "I... I used her. I manipulated her. I said whatever I needed to say to keep her from leaving. And when she stayed, I—" His voice cracked, and he looked down at his trembling hands. "I hurt her. Over and over again."

His mind flashed to the last fight they had before she walked out for good. She had been standing by the door, her bag slung over her shoulder, tears streaming down her face. *"Do you even love me, Vivhaan?"* she had asked, her voice breaking. He had scoffed, bitterness laced in his tone. *"Love you? I've done nothing but put up with your constant nagging and your endless need to fix me. Maybe you're the problem, Maya. Did you ever think of that?"*

The memory blurred in his mind, but the look on her face was crystal clear—shattered, as if he had taken a hammer to her heart.

"I said things I didn't mean," Vivhaan continued in the circle, his voice choked with emotion. "I said things to hurt her, to control her, because I was scared of losing her. But I lost her anyway. And now... now she has nothing left to believe in when it comes to me."

The counselor leaned forward, her voice steady but firm. "So, I'll ask again. What are you willing to do to make things right?"

Vivhaan wiped at his eyes, his jaw tightening. "I don't know if I can ever make it right," he admitted. "But I'll spend the rest of my life trying. Not just for her... but for me. Because if I don't change, then everything she went through—everything I put her through—it'll all mean nothing."

The room was silent as his words hung in the air. For the first time in years, Vivhaan wasn't running from his mistakes. He was staring them down, raw and unfiltered, and finally, he was ready to face them.

The Road To Rediscovery

One Saturday morning, Maya woke up with the sun streaming through her windows. It was a clear day, with the kind of crisp air that made her feel alive, refreshed. She stood by her window for a few moments, feeling the quiet rush of serenity in her chest. For the first time in a long while, there was no overwhelming sense of dread or anxiety about what the day might bring. There was only peace.

*****

The first thing on Maya's to-do list that day was a trip to the bookstore. It had been far too long since she had wandered through the aisles, searching for something to immerse herself in. Books had always been her escape, her therapy. She loved the smell of paper, the weight of a good book in her hands, and the way words could transport her to another world.

Walking into the bookstore felt like coming home. The shelves were stacked high with stories waiting to be discovered, each one a different adventure, a new life. As Maya roamed through the aisles, her fingers brushing the spines, she felt a sense of calm settle over her. She wasn't looking for anything in particular, but the process of browsing always had a grounding effect on her.

Her eyes landed on a book—one she had read before, but it seemed to call to her today. It was a book about healing, self-discovery, and the journey back to oneself. Maya smiled to herself and pulled it off the shelf. It felt like a sign. She knew it was exactly what she needed.

*****

Later that evening, sitting in her living room with the book open on her lap, Maya felt a surge of motivation. The words on the page spoke to her, reminding her that healing was not a linear process. There would be setbacks, difficult days, and moments of doubt, but it was all part of the journey. What mattered was that she kept moving forward. She didn't have to have everything figured out—she just had to keep taking steps, no matter how small.

As she read, her mind drifted back to Vivhaan. Even though she had made the decision to walk away, there were still days when the weight of the past pressed heavily on her chest. She missed him, yes, but she also missed the idea of what they had been. She missed the hope that things could change, the belief that love was enough to fix anything. But Maya knew now that love alone wasn't enough. She couldn't fix him. She couldn't carry him. She could only fix herself, and that was what she had to focus on.

*****

Maya's journey was not about erasing the past. She didn't want to forget what had happened. She wanted to remember the lessons, to take the pain and turn it into something meaningful. She wasn't going to be a victim of her circumstances. She was going to be the survivor who used her story to help others.

She started journaling every night, pouring her heart out onto the pages. At first, it was difficult. There were so many emotions she had kept bottled up for so long—anger, confusion, sadness. But as the days passed, the writing became a release. It was her way of processing everything she had been through, of untangling the emotions that had once been a tangled mess inside her.

Through her writing, Maya began to realize something important: she was stronger than she had ever given herself credit for. She had endured so much—emotional manipulation, gaslighting, the fear that she would never be enough—but she was still here. And that meant something. She had survived. And now, she was thriving.

*****

One evening, Maya ran into Ayesha at a local café. It had been a few weeks since their last catch-up, and Maya couldn't wait to share everything that had been going on in her life. They sat across from each other, steaming mugs of coffee in front of them, and Maya launched into her update.

"I've been doing a lot of thinking lately," Maya began, stirring her coffee absentmindedly. "About everything that happened with Vivhaan, but also about myself. I feel like I'm starting to figure things out. It's not perfect, but I'm in a better place. I don't feel so lost anymore."

Ayesha raised an eyebrow and took a sip of her latte, giving her a sly look. "Well, it's about time you caught up to what

I've been telling you for years," she said, half-teasing, half-serious.

Maya smiled sheepishly, her cheeks flushing. "I know. You were right, Ayesh. You were right about everything. And I'm sorry. For all those times I defended him, for the fights we had when you were just trying to look out for me. I should've listened to you."

Ayesha leaned back in her chair, her expression softening. "Maya, I'm not saying 'I told you so'—though, let's be honest, I totally could." She smirked before reaching across the table to squeeze Maya's hand. "But seriously, I never needed an apology. I just wanted you to see what I saw all along: how amazing you are and how much you deserve better than that loser."

Maya's eyes welled up, but she quickly blinked the tears away. "I feel so stupid for fighting with you about him. Remember that night at my place when you told me he was using me, and I just... I lost it? I said things I didn't mean, and I hate that I put him before you."

Ayesha waved her off. "Oh, trust me, I remember. You basically threw me out of your apartment and told me I didn't understand your relationship. It hurt, yeah, but I also knew you weren't ready to hear it. Sometimes you've gotta hit rock bottom before you can climb out, you know?"

Maya nodded slowly, the memory of that night coming back to her vividly. She had been so defensive, so desperate to believe in Vivhaan, that she had pushed away the one person who had always been there for her. "I owe you so much, Ayesha. You stuck by me even when I didn't deserve it."

Ayesha rolled her eyes, but her tone was gentle. "Maya, stop. You don't owe me anything. That's what friends do—they stick around, even when their best friend is being a complete idiot." She grinned, making Maya laugh despite herself. "But let me say this, and you better take it seriously: No more falling for idiots like him. You're done with fixer-upper projects, okay? You're not some emotional renovation service."

Maya chuckled, nodding. "Okay, okay. No more projects. Just... me."

"Exactly," Ayesha said firmly. "And don't think for a second that this is about you not being good enough or strong enough. Vivhaan didn't deserve you, Maya. He had no idea what to do with someone like you, so he tried to pull you down to his level. That's not love, that's insecurity."

Maya stared at her friend, her heart swelling with gratitude. "How do you always know exactly what to say?"

"Years of dealing with you," Ayesha teased. Then her tone softened again. "Look, Maya, I'm proud of you. I really am. You're doing the hard work, and it shows. But don't spend too much time looking back, okay? You've already lived through that mess. Now it's time to focus on what's ahead."

Maya smiled, a real, genuine smile. "You're right. Again."

"Always am," Ayesha quipped, raising her mug in a mock toast. "Here's to never settling for idiots, and to moving forward like the queen you are."

Maya laughed and clinked her mug against Ayesha's. "To moving forward."

And in that moment, surrounded by the warmth of her best friend's love and the comforting buzz of the café, Maya felt something she hadn't in a long time—hope.

*****

One morning, as Maya looked in the mirror, she saw the reflection of someone she didn't recognize. She looked different—not just physically, but emotionally. Her face held a quiet strength, a resilience that came from surviving the storm. And for the first time in a long while, Maya felt proud of the woman staring back at her.

She was no longer the woman who had clung to a broken relationship, hoping it would be fixed. She was the woman who had walked away, the woman who had chosen herself. And that was enough.

The Calm After the Storm

It had been months since Vivhaan had returned from rehab, and Maya's life had steadily moved forward. The heavy weight she had carried for so long had begun to lift, replaced by an overwhelming sense of peace she hadn't realized she'd been craving. She spent her days immersed in work, yoga, and reading, finding solace in the simple rhythms of life.

Her family had become a mix of cheerleaders, drill sergeants, and occasional interrogators in her journey to healing. They checked in often—sometimes too often—but their concern was wrapped in love and the kind of blunt honesty only family can provide.

*****

Her Father

One evening, as they sat on the balcony of her parents' house, her father handed her a cup of tea and leaned back in his chair, giving her a look that Maya knew all too well. It was the "you're not off the hook yet" look.

"So, Maya," he began, swirling his tea dramatically, "do I even *want* to know what all those years of me teaching you about self-respect, boundaries, and not putting up with nonsense were for? Because clearly, all my hard work has gone straight down the drain."

Maya groaned, rolling her eyes. "Dad, I get it. I messed up. You don't have to keep bringing it up."

"Oh, I absolutely do," he replied, his voice dripping with sarcasm. "Let's recap, shall we? I taught you how to spot red flags. I gave you a detailed manual—complete with diagrams—on how men should treat you. And what do you do? You go and date someone who probably had a flashing neon sign saying, 'Warning: Emotional Baggage Ahead.'"

Maya laughed despite herself. "Okay, okay! You've made your point."

He softened, his sarcasm giving way to concern. "Listen, kiddo. All jokes aside, I just want you to remember who you are. You're Maya—smart, strong, and way too good to let anyone dim your shine. Don't forget that. And don't let anyone else make you forget it, either."

"I won't, Dad," she said, her voice quieter now.

"Good," he said, leaning back with a smug smile. "Because if you do, I'm giving your future partners a printed copy of that manual. Maybe they'll take it more seriously than you did."

*****

Her Brother

Her brother, Rohan, was even less delicate. During dinner one night, he set down his fork with a loud clink and gave her a mock-serious look.

"So, let me get this straight," he began, his tone dripping with sarcasm. "You, Maya Sharma, the queen of calling out idiots and making them cry, dated *that guy*? And stayed with him? For *years*? Should I be worried about aliens controlling your brain, or was this just a temporary lapse in judgment?"

Maya sighed, stabbing a piece of broccoli with her fork. "It wasn't that simple, Rohan."

"Of course it wasn't," he said, leaning back dramatically. "It never is with you. But seriously, Maya, what the hell were you thinking? You're the person who used to roast guys for sending bad texts, and now I hear you were playing therapist to some dude who didn't deserve even five minutes of your time?"

She glared at him, but there was no real heat in it. "I wasn't 'playing therapist.' I thought I could help him. I thought—"

"That he'd change? That you'd fix him?" Rohan interrupted, his sarcasm giving way to exasperation. "Maya, you're not a miracle worker. You're my sister. And my sister doesn't settle for scraps. You hear me?"

Maya softened, the sting of his words replaced by the warmth of his concern. "I hear you. And for the record, I've learned my lesson."

"Good," he said, picking up his fork again. "Because if you ever pull something like this again, I swear, I'll beat you up myself. And then I'll go find the guy and beat him up, too. Equal opportunity justice."

*****

Her Sister-in-Law

In the kitchen, her sister-in-law, Nidhi, was less sarcastic but just as relentless. "Maya," she said, arms crossed as she leaned against the counter, "I love you, but I have to ask—what were you thinking? And why didn't you tell me what was really going on?"

Maya hesitated, chopping vegetables in silence for a moment. "I don't know. I guess... I thought I could handle it on my own."

"And how did that work out for you?" Nidhi asked, her tone pointed but not unkind.

"Not great," Maya admitted with a small laugh.

Nidhi softened, stepping closer. "Look, I get it. We all have our blind spots. But next time—because there better not be a next time—you need to trust me. I'm here for you, Maya. Always. Even when you're being stubborn and trying to do everything on your own."

Maya smiled, the weight of her sister-in-law's words sinking in. "Thanks, Nidhi. I'll remember that."

"Good," Nidhi said, pulling her into a quick hug. "And for the record, if you ever let someone treat you like that again, I'll be the first one to drag you out of there. No questions asked."

*****

Her Mother

Then came her mother's phone call one quiet Saturday morning. Maya picked up the phone, already bracing herself.

"Maya," her mother began, her voice warm but hesitant. "I've been thinking about you. I just want to know how you're doing."

"I'm fine, Mom," Maya replied, keeping her tone steady.

There was a pause, and then her mother's voice dropped, sharp with concern. "I just... I hope you haven't spoken to Vivhaan. Tell me you haven't, Maya."

Maya felt a surge of tension in her chest. "Mom, I haven't. I told you, I don't want to talk about him anymore."

Her mother's relief was short-lived, replaced quickly by a simmering fury. "Good. Because if you had, I'd have lost my mind. Do you honestly think I'd ever want you to speak to that... that *man* again? After everything he put you through? I hope you understand, Maya, I can't even *stand* the thought of him having any part of your life. You owe him nothing. He deserves nothing but your anger—and mine."

Maya closed her eyes, the weight of her mother's words sinking in. "I get it, Mom. I've moved on. I won't let him drag me back into that."

Her mother's voice grew even more fierce. "You better not. Because I swear, if I see him even *think* about coming near you, I'll—" She stopped herself, her protective rage barely contained. "Maya, you're better off without him. I won't have you wasting another second on someone who treated you like garbage."

Maya smiled faintly, comforted by her mother's unwavering support. "I know, Mom. I'm really okay. I'm happier than I've been in years."

Her mother sighed, the sharpness leaving her voice but not her protective tone. "I'm just so glad to hear that, sweetie. Don't let anyone—*especially* him—ever make you forget how amazing you are. No one deserves to make you feel small, least of all him."

"I won't forget, Mom. I promise," Maya said, her voice strong.

Through her family's sarcasm, tough love, and unwavering support, Maya found the strength to keep moving forward. They reminded her of who she was—strong, independent, and capable of building a life that was hers alone. And for the first time in years, she believed it, too.

*****

Later that evening, Maya sat down with a cup of tea in her cozy apartment, looking out the window at the city lights. It was a quiet night, but it was hers. There was no chaos, no fear, no one else's needs to put before her own. It was just her and the life she had reclaimed. She had found something she thought was lost—herself.

Her phone buzzed, interrupting her peaceful moment. Maya picked it up, expecting a message from a friend or maybe a work-related update. But instead, it was a notification from Vivhaan.

I miss you, Maya. I still think about you every day. I don't know if I'll ever be able to make things right, but I want you to know that I'll never stop trying.

Maya stared at the screen for a moment, her heart skipping a beat. She had heard these words before, many times. They had once held so much power over her, a mix of hope and despair. But now, they felt empty. Hollow. She had walked away for a reason—because she deserved more than apologies that came too late.

With a steady hand, she put the phone down. She didn't need to respond. She didn't owe him anything. Not anymore.

And so, with a deep breath and a quiet smile, Maya embraced the stillness of the night, ready to continue building the life she had dreamed of.

The Unexpected Encounter

It was a sunny afternoon when Maya walked into her favorite café, a quiet place with old wooden tables and the scent of freshly brewed coffee lingering in the air. She had been working on a new project, her mind buzzing with creative ideas, and needed a break. She ordered her usual—a chai latte—and found a cozy spot by the window. As she sipped the warm drink, letting the moment settle into the rhythm of her breath, Maya felt a strange peace that had eluded her for years. She was finally at peace with herself.

She had become someone new—stronger, sharper, more self-aware. She had rebuilt her life, piece by piece, and was no longer the woman who second-guessed her worth or believed she had to settle for a relationship that drained her. Vivhaan was part of a life she had left behind, and she had no intention of looking back.

But then, the door opened, and the familiar sound of her name pulled her out of her thoughts.

"Maya?"

She froze.

There was no mistaking that voice. Deep, rich, with the kind of warmth that once made her feel like she was home. Vivhaan.

Her heart skipped, but she didn't move. She didn't need to. She remained rooted in place, a slight tension in her chest, but no longer in the tight grip of his presence. She had changed. The old Maya—the one who would have jumped to her feet, confused and torn—was gone.

Vivhaan stepped into her line of sight, and she felt the years between them in the air. He looked the same, but also different. His face was a little more worn, his eyes carrying the weight of experience, regret, and something else—guilt? Longing?

His eyes scanned the café, a familiar hope flickering in them, until they found her. And when they did, something in him seemed to deflate.

"Maya," he said, his voice catching slightly, "I... I didn't expect to see you here."

Maya didn't flinch. She didn't acknowledge the years of pain, the heartache, the broken promises. She simply looked up at him, calm and unwavering, as if he was a ghost—a shadow of someone who once meant everything to her.

"Vivhaan," she said, her tone flat, controlled. "What are you doing here?"

His eyes softened for a moment. He took a step closer, his gaze searching hers, looking for the woman he once knew. The woman who would have softened, who would have given him the chance to explain.

"I was passing by," he said, but there was no conviction in his words. "I... thought I might find you here."

Maya's lips curled slightly in what could almost be a smile, but it wasn't one of warmth. It was one of quiet resolve. She took a deliberate sip of her chai, her eyes never leaving his. She had no need for theatrics. She had learned the hard way how to let things go, and Vivhaan was a chapter that had closed long ago.

She set the cup down slowly, then met his eyes, her voice cool, edged with something sharp. "I didn't expect to see you either."

Vivhaan flinched. He wasn't prepared for this—this distance, this indifference. He'd imagined this moment a thousand times, each time with hope, with the idea that somehow Maya would still be there, waiting for him. But what stood before him now was a woman who had shed the skin of the past, a woman who was no longer tethered to him or the memory of what they had once been.

He took a deep breath, the words spilling out in a rush, as if he had been carrying them for too long. "I just wanted to... apologize. I know I can't undo what happened, but I need you to know that I regret it. Everything. The way I treated you. The way I... didn't appreciate you." He paused, searching for something in her eyes, but found only quiet strength. "I've been working on myself, Maya. I've been trying. I just... I don't know what I was thinking back then, but I regret it all."

Maya didn't respond immediately. She felt a sharp sting, but it wasn't for him. It was for the version of herself she had once been—the one who had clung to a man who never deserved her. She could see his sincerity, but sincerity wasn't enough anymore. It hadn't been enough before.

"I'm glad you're working on yourself," Maya said, her voice calm, but there was an unmistakable edge to it now, cutting through the air between them. "But I need you to hear this, Vivhaan: I don't need you to fix yourself for me. I walked away for a reason. I was never your project to fix. You couldn't give me what I needed, and I'm not going back to that. You're not part of my life anymore."

Vivhaan's face tightened, his jaw clenching as if the words were punching him in the gut. He opened his mouth, but no words came out. He had come here hoping for some kind of redemption, but instead, he was faced with the finality of her words. The coldness was overwhelming, the realization sinking deep into him like a stone.

"I don't know what else to say," he mumbled, voice hoarse, "but I... I just wanted you to know how sorry I am."

Maya's eyes locked onto his, and her gaze was as cold as ice. There was no sympathy, no warmth. He was a stranger to her now, someone who had once been a part of her life but no longer held any space in it. She looked at him as if he never existed, as if he had been a mere footnote in the story of her life, easily erased.

"You don't need to say anything," Maya replied, her voice crisp, sharp. "You've said enough. I've spent years forgiving you in my head. You don't get to take up any more of my time. You're just... done. Understand?"

The finality in her tone hit him like a slap. For a moment, he didn't know what to do, but before he could speak again, the door to the café opened, and a familiar voice cut through the tension.

"Vivhaan?" A sharp, angry voice.

Maya didn't flinch. She didn't even look in the direction of the door.

Her best friend, Aria, had walked in, her face flushed with anger. She was someone Maya had confided in during the darkest moments of her past, someone who had watched Vivhaan tear Maya apart and who had been waiting for this very moment to see him crash. Aria's eyes landed on Vivhaan, and for a second, her anger flared—but she didn't look at him again. Not directly.

Aria's gaze turned to Maya, and the look of understanding passed between them—Maya didn't need to react to Vivhaan. It was as if he had never existed.

Vivhaan watched this exchange, his face twisting with confusion and hurt. He opened his mouth to speak to Aria, to apologize or say something—anything—but Aria walked past him, ignoring him completely, and made her way to Maya. She leaned down and whispered in Maya's ear, loud enough for Vivhaan to hear, but not acknowledge him.

"Are you okay?" Aria asked, her voice steady, like Vivhaan didn't matter.

Maya nodded, her face still impassive. "I'm fine."

Vivhaan stood there, watching Maya and Aria, feeling a strange, crushing weight settle on his chest. He had come in seeking closure, some thread of connection, but what he found was a woman who had utterly erased him. He wasn't even a blip in her existence anymore.

And that realization shattered him.

Maya's eyes flicked toward him for a brief moment before she stood up, no longer looking back at him. "Goodbye, Vivhaan," she said, the words cold and final, like an executioner's sentence. "Don't come looking for me again."

With that, she walked away with Aria, leaving Vivhaan standing there, a man undone by the emptiness of her gaze, his heart breaking under the weight of a truth he couldn't escape. Maya was gone—completely gone from his life.

It was strange to realize that someone who had once meant the world to her now felt like he never existed at all.

The Ripple Effect

It had been a few weeks since Vivhaan's unexpected appearance, and while Maya had pushed the encounter to the back of her mind, a lingering quietness had settled over her. The memories of him still surfaced from time to time—especially in those rare, still moments when she allowed herself to think about the life she had left behind. But the truth was, she didn't miss him. Not really. She missed the version of herself that she had been before everything spiraled out of control—the confident, carefree woman who loved herself fiercely. That version was starting to reemerge.

She had spent years trying to be someone she wasn't—trying to fit herself into a relationship that was never meant to be. Now, Maya was learning to rebuild herself on her own terms.

Maya sat in her favorite park, a quiet spot where the trees whispered and the wind played gently through the leaves. It was her refuge, a place she went to whenever she needed to reconnect with herself. Today, she had brought her journal, the one filled with sketches, scribbles, and thoughts that helped her understand her own heart. She hadn't written much lately, her mind too occupied with the turbulence of the past. But now, in the stillness, she felt the pull to write again.

As she flipped open the journal, her mind wandered back to the months she had spent with Vivhaan. Those were the moments she had hoped to forget, but now, looking at them from a distance, she was able to see them with a clearer, softer lens. The pain was still there, but it wasn't the sharp, unrelenting ache it once was. Instead, it had softened, becoming part of her story, a chapter that had led her to where she was now.

Maya's pen moved across the paper, her words flowing freely: *"I used to think love was about what we gave to each other, how we made each other better. But now I know that love starts with what you give to yourself, how you honor who you are before anyone else ever has the chance to. I am learning to love myself in ways I never thought possible."*

She paused, looking up at the sky. The clouds were drifting lazily, and the sun cast its golden light over the park. She had spent so much of her life trying to be loved, to fit into someone else's idea of happiness. But now, Maya understood that real freedom came when she loved herself first. When she stopped waiting for someone else's approval or validation.

As the days went on, Maya found herself focusing more on the things that brought her joy—writing, painting, hiking, and spending time with friends who genuinely cared for her. She rekindled her passion for art, something she had buried deep inside herself during the chaos of her relationship with Vivhaan. Her work began to evolve, and with it, so did her confidence. She was no longer the woman who sought validation in toxic love; she was the woman who stood firm in her own truth.

But despite the newfound peace she had found, there was an undeniable emptiness that lingered in the background. The weight of her past decisions still hung around her like a fog—quiet, but persistent. She had made peace with her relationship with Vivhaan, but the aftershocks of it still rippled through her life.

One afternoon, as she sat at a café writing, her phone buzzed. It was a message from an unknown number. Her heart skipped a beat as she read the words:

"Maya, it's Vivhaan. I've been thinking a lot about what we talked about, and I wanted to check in on you. I hope you're doing well."

Her thumb hovered over the screen as a million thoughts raced through her mind. She had worked so hard to get to a place where she wasn't constantly haunted by his presence, by his words. Part of her wanted to ignore the message, to continue living in the world she had created for herself. But there was also a part of her that wanted closure, even if it came in a form she hadn't expected.

Maya took a deep breath and replied:

"I'm doing well, Vivhaan. Thank you for checking in. I'm glad to hear you're doing better. I've moved on, but I appreciate your message."

She hit send and immediately felt a sense of relief. There was no desire to revisit the past, no longing to reopen old wounds.

She had closed that chapter for good, and now, she was living for herself.

Later that evening, as Maya sat on her balcony, watching the sun dip below the horizon, she reflected on how far she had come. Her journey was no longer defined by a toxic relationship. She wasn't waiting for anyone else to make her whole. She had become whole on her own.

And then, as if the universe was affirming her decision, Maya received a call from her best friend, Sara.

"Yo, Maya, what the hell is wrong with you?" Sara's voice was teasing but sharp, carrying that familiar blend of affection and exasperation. "I just got your message, and honestly, I'm about to lose my mind. Why the hell would you reply to that idiot?"

Maya paused, a small smile tugging at her lips. "What's up, Sara? Why are you acting like I killed someone?"

"Are you serious right now? You're not even mad? I thought you were done with him for good." There was a pause, and Maya could hear Sara let out a dramatic sigh. "You literally sent him a thank-you note for checking in? Maya, you are an idiot. He didn't deserve a single word from you, especially not 'I've moved on.' Seriously, what were you thinking?"

Maya laughed softly, her tone calm but a little defensive. "I wasn't thinking, Sara. I just wanted to make sure he knew that I was fine. That's it."

Sara groaned. "Fine? You want to be fine, or you want to be free? Let me break it down for you. The only thing that idiot needs to hear from you is nothing. Silence. You don't owe him an explanation or even a 'I've moved on' speech. You're done. Period. And the sooner you cut that emotional tie, the better. That's the real 'moving on,' not playing nice with him."

Maya nodded, even though Sara couldn't see her. She knew her friend was right. "You're right. I just... I don't know, I thought I should be the bigger person."

Sara laughed, but it wasn't a happy sound. "The bigger person? Are you kidding me? No, no, Maya. You've been the bigger person for years, putting up with that mess. Now, it's time to be the smart person. Don't give him a single second of your energy. He's gone. Let him stay gone."

Maya felt the familiar weight of Sara's words settle over her, grounding her, and for the first time in a while, she felt a little lighter. "You're right, Sara. I'll do better next time. No more giving him space in my head or heart."

"Damn straight," Sara replied, her voice softer now. "You've got so much better ahead of you. Trust me, you're already living a better life. Just don't go backwards."

The call ended, and Maya sat for a moment, absorbing the conversation. She realized Sara was right—she didn't need to explain herself to anyone, especially not to Vivhaan. She had walked away for a reason. The more she focused on herself and her own growth, the less space he had in her world.

And with that, Maya took a deep breath, looking out over the horizon. She was ready for the next chapter. For the first time in a long time, she didn't feel the need to rush. She was savoring the moment, knowing that the future was hers to create.

The Strength of Silence

Vivhaan stood at the edge of the balcony, gripping the railing so hard his knuckles turned white, the city lights below blurring into a haze. Everything around him felt so damn loud—people laughing, cars honking, the chatter of life—but inside, all he heard was the deafening silence of his own self-loathing. Weeks had passed since he reached out to Maya, and every second felt like a goddamn eternity. He had expected nothing, and yet he had expected everything. He wanted a sign that things might go back to how they were, that he could fix this—but no. The weight of his failure was sinking in deeper, suffocating him.

His head spun with regret, confusion, anger—so much anger. The alcohol was no longer a crutch. It was a disease. A slow poison. And no matter how much he drank, no matter how much he tried to drown the pain, it *never* went away. It just hung around, a gnawing presence, waiting for him to slip up. And god, he'd slipped up so many damn times.

"Maya," he growled under his breath, the name a bitter taste in his mouth. "She deserves so much better than this... than me."

The thought of her face, her kindness, her smile—he crushed those memories, smothered them with the weight of his failures. He had fucked it all up. She had been the one thing that had ever mattered to him, and he ruined it. Over and over.

His phone buzzed in his pocket, and the screen flashed his mother's name. A wave of heat flooded his chest, anger rising fast. He wanted to hurl the phone across the room. He didn't need her cold, disapproving messages. She didn't get it—*none of them did*. She had never seen him, never understood him. All she ever saw was a son who needed fixing, and all she ever did was remind him that he was a disappointment.

He snatched the phone out of his pocket and read her message, each word piercing through him like a thousand needles.

"Vivhaan. Rehab session tomorrow. You need to keep up. I don't want to hear any more excuses. How are you holding up?"

How am I holding up?

He could feel his fists clenching, his body trembling with frustration. How was he holding up? He was *falling apart*. And yet, she couldn't see it. She never could.

With shaking hands, he typed a quick, detached response. "I'm fine, Mom. Getting there. I'll be at the session tomorrow."

That was all. She didn't deserve more. He didn't want to give her the satisfaction of knowing how broken he really was. How lost.

Vivhaan slammed the phone down on the table, the anger boiling over now.

"Maya," he muttered, his voice barely a whisper, but thick with venom. "She thinks she's better off without me? Fine. Let her live her perfect little life. She was always too good for me anyway. And you know what? I *fucked it up*. I ruined her. And now... now she's gone. Gone, and I'm just here—stuck—wondering what the hell happened."

His thoughts spiraled, faster and faster, dragging him deeper into the pit of self-hatred. Every flaw, every weakness, every single fucking mistake he'd ever made came rushing to the surface. He couldn't escape it. His demons—his addiction, his pride, his anger—were suffocating him. And they were winning.

He grabbed the nearest bottle of whiskey, his hands shaking so violently that some of the liquid spilled over the edge of the glass. *It doesn't matter*, he thought bitterly. *Nothing matters. I don't matter.*

The bottle felt like the only thing that could numb him. The only thing that could quiet the storm inside. He raised it to his lips, but something in the back of his mind—a sliver of awareness—stopped him. The cold glass pressed against his mouth, and for a moment, he was about to give in. He was *this close* to slipping back into the haze.

But then—his phone buzzed again.

This time, it was his therapist.

"Vivhaan, I know it's tough, but you need to call me. I'm here. Don't let this moment swallow you whole. I know you're close, but you have to fight this."

Vivhaan stared at the screen, his mind racing. The temptation to ignore the message, to throw the phone away and bury himself in the bottle, was overwhelming. But that quiet voice—the voice he hadn't heard in ages—screamed at him to pick it up. To talk. To *do something* different for once.

His chest heaved with rage. "Fight this? Fight this?" he spat out loud. "I'm so fucking tired of fighting. What's the point? It never ends. It never gets better. Maya's gone. She's not coming back. *Nothing* is going to change."

He wanted to throw the phone across the room. He wanted to scream until his lungs gave out. He wanted to let the anger swallow him whole.

But that tiny sliver—the one that still fought to stay alive—pushed him. The phone. The therapist. The thought of *facing it*.

His breathing was ragged as he lowered the bottle, his eyes fixed on the phone. His entire body trembled with fury, every muscle clenched in the fight to hold himself together.

Finally, with a snarl, he answered.

"Yeah?" His voice was thick with bitterness, but he couldn't stop himself from picking up the phone. "What do you want?"

"Vivhaan," the therapist's voice came through, calm but firm. "I know you're angry. I know you're hurting. But this isn't the answer. You've got to stop hiding behind that anger. You've got to face it. I'm here. You don't have to do this alone."

He slammed his fist into the wall, the pain shooting up his arm, but he didn't care. "I'm done with this. Done with *her*, done with *you*... done with everything."

The therapist didn't back down. "Vivhaan, listen to me. You've been running for so long. But if you keep running, if you keep hiding from the truth, you're only going to drag yourself deeper into this pit. Maya's gone, yes. But you're still here. You can still fix this. You just have to want it."

Vivhaan slammed the phone against the wall, the glass shattering, and he let out a guttural scream. He wasn't ready for this. He didn't want to fight anymore. He just wanted the pain to stop. The anger, the regret, the guilt—it was all too much.

He grabbed the whiskey again, but this time, there was a fury in his movements. "Fuck it," he snarled, pouring himself another glass, the liquor sloshing over the rim. He was done. He was done trying. Maya was gone. He was lost. And nothing was going to change.

But just as he brought the glass to his lips again, the last sliver of clarity inside him flickered, fading, but still there. His chest tightened with desperation. He could feel the pull of the bottle, the safety of the numbness. But deep down, something screamed that this wasn't it. He had to decide—*now*.

Vivhaan paused, staring into the glass. The darkness was calling. And it was almost too easy to slip back into it.

But then, he felt the sharp sting of something else—*a choice*.

This wasn't the end. Not yet.

But damn, it was close.

Redemption Journey

Vivhaan sat back in the stiff, uncomfortable chair of Dr. Patel's office, staring at the floor as his mind drifted to places he wasn't ready to go. But here, with the quiet hum of the fluorescent lights and the weight of his own thoughts pressing down on him, he couldn't escape it.

Dr. Patel sat across from him, her eyes steady and calm as she waited for him to speak. The silence felt thick, heavy, like something unspoken hung in the air between them. Vivhaan's fingers twitched, a nervous habit he'd developed when the pressure of his own mind became too much. He hated this feeling—the feeling of being so far removed from the person he used to be, the person who hadn't ruined everything.

"Do you ever think about her?" Dr. Patel asked softly, almost cautiously.

Vivhaan clenched his jaw, the words she had spoken pulling him into a dark place he didn't want to go. He felt the weight of his chest tighten as the memories of Maya came crashing back.

"I think about her every damn day," he muttered, his voice barely above a whisper. He didn't look up, couldn't look up. It was like if he didn't, he could hide from the truth. The truth of what he had done.

Dr. Patel's voice was gentle, but insistent. **"What do you think about?"**

Vivhaan exhaled sharply, as though the air was too thick to breathe. He let his mind wander, replaying the moments in his head like a movie he couldn't turn off. He had been to rehab more times than he cared to count, but no matter how many steps forward he took, these memories always dragged him back to the same dark place. Maya was always there, haunting him.

He closed his eyes briefly, recalling their first date—the picnic.

"I remember the first time I saw her," Vivhaan began, the words coming out in a rush, like he needed to speak them aloud to make sense of them. **"She was so... full of life. So warm. I knew I wanted to be around her, to have her in my life. I thought I could be... someone better with her. And I tried—I swear, I tried. But it was like the moment she smiled at me, I started lying. I started showing her a version of myself I wasn't."**

Dr. Patel leaned forward slightly, her attention focused. **"What was the version of yourself you were showing her?"**

Vivhaan's hands tightened into fists, and his chest heaved as the weight of his own guilt threatened to crush him. **"The good version. The version who wasn't hiding behind a bottle. The guy who could make her laugh, who could hold her hand and tell her everything was going to be okay. The** guy who said, 'I love you,' and meant it, even though I had no idea what love was at that point. I was so damn good at pretending, at making her think I was who I said I was. But it was all a lie."

His voice cracked as the weight of those words hit him. He could see it—the picnic under the tree, the way Maya had looked at him, the way she had trusted him. She had given him everything, all of herself, and he had taken it and destroyed it piece by piece.

"I can still see her face, you know?" Vivhaan's voice faltered. "The way she looked when I made that picnic for her. She was so happy. It was like I had given her the world, and she was so grateful for it. And I thought... I thought I was doing the right thing. I thought if I gave her that, she would see the real me, the guy I was trying to be."

Dr. Patel's voice was measured but firm. "But you weren't being the real you, were you?"

Vivhaan's throat tightened, the weight of the truth almost too much to bear. "No. I wasn't. I wasn't even close." He ran a hand through his hair, frustration bubbling up inside him. "I thought I could be that guy, the one she needed. But I kept slipping back into the old habits, the old ways of coping. The drinking, the anger, the lies. I thought I could hide it from her, that she wouldn't see it. But she did. She saw through all of it."

His mind flashed back to the last conversation they had before he went to rehab. Her face was a mixture of exhaustion and resolve, like she had already made up her mind. She had finally seen through the facade, and it had destroyed him.

"I can still hear her," he murmured, voice breaking. "The way she told me it was over. Like she was giving up on me, but at the same time... I knew it was me who had given up on her first."

Dr. Patel didn't say anything, just let him talk. She knew this was part of the process—letting the anger, the guilt, the regret surface so he could confront it.

"I used her, you know," Vivhaan said suddenly, his voice harsh with self-loathing. "She had this... energy about her, this way of making people feel seen, making them feel like they mattered. I didn't deserve that. But I used it. I let her believe I was someone I wasn't because it was easier that way. She gave me everything, and I just took it. I made her think I was this guy she could fix, this guy she could save. But I was never worth saving."

Dr. Patel's voice softened, but there was an edge to it. "What do you think she saw in you?"

Vivhaan shook his head, unable to answer right away. The question felt like a punch to the gut. What had she seen in him? Was it love? Or was it just the need to fix someone who was broken beyond repair?

"She saw someone worth loving. She saw someone who could change, who could be better. And maybe, deep down, I wanted to be that person for her. But every time I tried, I just... failed. I let her down. And now, all I have left are the broken pieces of what could have been."

Dr. Patel's gaze didn't waver. "So, what now? What are you going to do with those broken pieces?"

Vivhaan fell silent, the weight of his own guilt crushing him. For a moment, he thought of picking up the bottle again. The thought came unbidden, a fleeting impulse. The numbness, the escape—it all seemed so damn easy. He could drown everything in liquor, forget all of this... forget her. But then, just as quickly as the thought entered his mind, something else stopped him.

His phone buzzed.

Vivhaan glanced down, his breath catching in his throat. It was a message from his mother—a simple reminder about the next rehab session. The weight of his choices, the guilt, the anger—it all collided inside him.

He wanted to scream. He wanted to throw the phone across the room and go back to the life he knew, the one where nothing mattered, where the alcohol took away the pain. But instead, he gripped the phone tightly in his hand, the anger simmering beneath the surface. He wasn't sure if he could do this. He wasn't sure if he could change. But for the first time in months, he felt something—a tiny spark of hope.

Dr. Patel's voice broke through the fog in his mind. **"You don't have to do this alone, Vivhaan. But you have to choose to change. The road won't be easy, but it's the only way forward."**

Vivhaan stared at the phone in his hand, the weight of the decision pressing down on him. For the first time in a long time, he felt the faintest stirrings of hope. Maybe he could rebuild. Maybe, just maybe, he could find a way to make things right—starting with himself.

Maya on the other hand had spent weeks focusing solely on her work, on building the life she had almost forgotten she wanted. Every morning, she would wake up, not to the anxiety of the past but to the hope of her future. The days blurred into one another as she found her rhythm again. But there were times when the weight of her memories would come crashing in—like waves against jagged rocks.

It had been weeks since Vivhaan's phone call, since he had gone to rehab, and since she had made the decision to walk away from him. She had stood firm in her decision, despite the doubts and emotional pull of the past. But deep down, Maya knew she was no longer the woman who had entered that toxic relationship. She had rediscovered the parts of herself she had hidden away, the parts that had gotten lost in Vivhaan's chaos.

One afternoon, after a busy day at the office, Maya found herself sitting on her balcony, staring out at the city skyline. She thought about everything she had been through—the late-night conversations, the laughter, the arguments, and the pain. And yet, she realized that it wasn't just about the relationship with Vivhaan. It was about how she had allowed herself to become someone else for the sake of that relationship.

She had forgotten how to be her authentic self.

The quiet moments she now spent alone, rediscovering the things she loved—painting, reading, yoga—were beginning to fill her up in a way she hadn't realized she needed. She had always been independent, always been a go-getter, but Vivhaan had somehow made her forget that.

Her laughter was no longer held back by insecurities, her smile no longer stifled by shame. She had reclaimed her voice, and it was stronger than ever. But there were moments, fleeting moments, when she felt the weight of the loss. The dreams they had once shared together now felt like ghosts.

Maya had always been a romantic at heart, and part of her still wished things could have turned out differently. But as time passed, she realized that walking away had been the hardest, but the best, decision she had ever made.

She needed to focus on her own healing, her own growth. She deserved a love that uplifted her, not one that drained her. And that love started with herself.

The Final Goodbye

Vivhaan had been in a constant battle with himself. The hours in therapy, the nights spent thinking about Maya and the wreckage he had caused, all weighed heavily on his mind. He knew he couldn't erase the past, and some wounds were too deep to heal quickly. But he had to try, for his own redemption, and for any possibility of rebuilding what they once had.

Each day, the thought of Maya lingered in his thoughts, an overwhelming presence he couldn't shake. He didn't expect forgiveness, but he desperately wanted to show her that he had changed, that he was no longer the man who had hurt her. But the fear of rejection kept him paralyzed, unsure whether reaching out would cause more harm than good. He didn't know if she was even ready to hear from him, or if she ever would be. But his desire to make things right remained constant, like a fire that wouldn't go out.

It was late one evening when he sat at his desk, phone in hand, staring at the draft of the text message he had written countless times. Each version had been deleted. Each attempt had felt insufficient. But tonight, he felt a shift inside him. He was ready.

He took a deep breath and hit send.

Hey Maya,

I know I don't deserve your time or forgiveness, but I've been thinking a lot about you. About us. I've spent the last few months working on myself, trying to understand the damage I caused. I'm not asking you to forgive me, but I wanted you to know that I'm genuinely sorry for everything. I was selfish, toxic, and I hurt you in ways I can never take back.

If you ever want to talk, I'm here. No pressure, no expectations. Just wanted you to know that I'm doing better, and I'll always care about you.

Vivhaan

*****

The silence after Vivhaan's message had been deafening. The hours stretched into days, and Maya couldn't bring herself to respond. She had spent so much time reliving their relationship, replaying the pain and the heartbreak, that even the simplest decision felt monumental. She wasn't sure if she was ready to hear his voice again, to revisit the past that had nearly destroyed her.

But then, one morning, the phone rang. Vivhaan's name flashed across the screen, and for a moment, Maya's heart stopped. It was a moment she had both anticipated and feared, a moment that threatened to unravel everything she had worked so hard to build.

She hesitated, her hand hovering over the screen. Should she answer? Should she ignore it? Could she even handle another conversation with him? Her mind raced, but one thing became clear: this call, whether she wanted it or not, was inevitable.

With a shaky breath, she pressed the green button.

"Hello?" she said, her voice controlled, though her heart thudded in her chest.

"Maya," Vivhaan's voice came through the phone, softer than she remembered, trembling with vulnerability. There was a long pause, the silence heavy with unspoken words. "I... I didn't think you'd pick up."

Maya hesitated, her fingers tightening around the phone. She hadn't expected to hear his voice again, and yet, here it was, pulling her back into a past she had worked so hard to leave behind. "I wasn't sure either," she said finally, her tone guarded but not unkind.

The silence between them felt like an eternity, the kind of silence where both were unsure of what to say or where to go next. Finally, Vivhaan spoke again, breaking the tension.

"Thank you for picking up," he said quietly. "I've wanted to talk to you for so long, but I didn't know how to reach out without causing you more pain."

Maya's grip on the phone tightened as old memories rose to the surface. The pain, the anger, the exhaustion of trying to make it work, all threatened to overwhelm her. But she held herself steady.

"Vivhaan, you hurt me more than I ever thought I could be hurt," she said, the words bitter in her mouth. "It's not something you can fix with a text or a phone call."

"I know," he responded quickly, his voice thick with emotion. "I'm not calling to ask for forgiveness or to make excuses. I just... I need you to know how sorry I am. For everything. For the person I was, for the way I treated you. I've been in therapy, working through everything, and... Maya, I don't even recognize who I was back then."

His words were laced with pain, and for a moment, Maya could almost believe them. The person he had been—the person who had hurt her, controlled her, made her feel small—felt like someone she had never truly known. But the scars were still there, etched deep into her heart.

"Why now, Vivhaan?" she asked, her voice sharp with the edge of frustration. "Why are you calling me now, after all this time?"

"Because I couldn't live with myself if I didn't try to make amends," he confessed. "You were the best thing that ever happened to me, and I destroyed it. I destroyed us. I needed you to know that I see that now. I'm not the same person anymore."

Maya's chest tightened at his words. For a moment, a flicker of hope stirred in her, a fleeting desire to believe that things could have been different. But she quickly crushed it. She couldn't let herself go back down that road.

"Do you think that changes anything?" she asked bitterly. "Do you think an apology undoes all the pain you caused? Do you think it erases the nights I spent wondering what I did wrong?

The nights I cried myself to sleep because I felt so worthless, so small?"

"No," he said quietly, his voice full of regret. "I don't think it erases anything. And I'll carry the weight of what I did for the rest of my life. But I want you to know it wasn't your fault. None of it was your fault."

Maya's breath caught in her throat. She had blamed herself for so long, wondering if she had somehow been too much, too emotional, too demanding. Hearing him say those words, hearing him take responsibility in a way he never had before, cracked something open inside her. She hadn't realized just how much she needed to hear that.

"Vivhaan," she said after a long pause, her voice trembling but firm, "I'm glad you're getting help. I truly am. But I've spent so much time trying to rebuild myself after you tore me apart. I've worked so hard to get my life back without you in it. I don't know if I can let you back in—not even for a conversation."

"I understand," he said, his voice thick with sadness. "And I don't expect anything from you, Maya. I just... I needed you to know that I'm sorry. And I'll spend the rest of my life trying to be better, even if you're not a part of it."

Maya's heart ached at his words. She wasn't ready to forgive him. She wasn't sure she ever would be. But something had shifted in her, something she hadn't expected. She had found the closure she had been searching for.

"Vivhaan," she said softly, "I hope you continue to work on yourself. I hope you find peace. But I also hope you understand that I can't go back to who I was when I was with you. I'm not her anymore."

"I wouldn't want you to," he replied sincerely. "You're stronger now, Maya. And I know I don't deserve it, but... thank you. Thank you for even taking this call."

Maya nodded, even though he couldn't see her. "Goodbye, Vivhaan."

"Goodbye, Maya," he whispered, and the finality in his voice told her everything she needed to know.

As she hung up the phone, Maya stood still for a long moment. The conversation had stirred up old wounds, but it had also given her the clarity she needed. She didn't know if she would ever fully forgive him, but for the first time, she felt like she could finally close the chapter on their relationship.

With a deep breath, she stepped out onto the balcony, the cool evening air soothing her. The weight in her chest was lighter now, and for the first time in what felt like forever, she allowed herself to smile. She was free.

Moving Forward

Maya hung up the phone, her hand lingering on it as though it carried the weight of the past. Her emotions were tangled, a mix of relief, anger, sadness, and a strange sense of liberation. Talking to Vivhaan had stirred up memories she had carefully compartmentalized—some tender, some so painful that they felt like fresh wounds. But now, as she sat in the quiet of her office, she realized something profound: she wasn't the same person she had been when she was with him.

A soft knock on the door startled her. She looked up to see Shaan standing in the doorway, a bouquet of lilies in his hand. His presence was a surprise, but not an unwelcome one. Shaan had always been a steady presence in her life, even during the darkest moments with Vivhaan.

She thought back to the first time they had met, at a friend's party years ago. He had been the one to make her laugh when she was feeling out of place, the one who had always been there to pick her up when she fell. Even during her relationship with Vivhaan, Shaan had never judged her, never pushed her to leave. He had simply been there, a quiet reminder that she was never truly alone.

"Hey," he said, his voice warm but tinged with concern. "I heard you were having a rough day. Thought you could use some flowers... and maybe some company."

Maya smiled faintly, the tension in her chest easing slightly. "You always know how to show up at the right time, don't you?"

Shaan shrugged, a playful grin tugging at his lips. "It's a gift. Now, are you going to let me in, or do I have to stand here all day?"

The Maya who had once been consumed by his love and chaos no longer existed. That Maya had been broken down, but from those pieces, a new Maya had emerged—stronger, wiser, and unwilling to compromise her worth for anyone. This phone call wasn't closure in the way she had expected. It wasn't the kind where you tie everything up neatly and move on without a backward glance. No, it was messy, raw, and complicated. But it was closure nonetheless.

She leaned back in her chair and glanced at the partially written document on her laptop screen. It was the opening chapter of her book, the one she had been pouring her heart into. Writing about her experiences had been like stitching herself back together. Each word was a thread, pulling her closer to a version of herself she had forgotten existed.

The book wasn't just about Vivhaan. It was about her—her journey, her resilience, her pain, and her growth. It was about the lessons she wished she had learned earlier and the hope she wanted to offer others who might be trapped in similar cycles. For the first time in years, she felt a sense of purpose that wasn't tied to someone else's validation. This was hers.

A soft knock on the door startled her. She looked up to see Asha, her assistant, poking her head into the room with a knowing smile.

"Maya, someone's here to see you," Asha said, her eyes sparkling with intrigue.

"Who is it?" Maya asked, frowning slightly. She wasn't expecting anyone.

"It's a surprise," Asha replied with a grin, stepping aside to let the visitor in.

Maya's breath caught as Shaan stepped into view. She hadn't seen him in months, not since a brief catch-up at a mutual friend's event. He was holding a bouquet of lilies and carnations, his expression warm but tinged with a hint of nervousness.

"Shaan," Maya said, standing up slowly. "What...what are you doing here?"

He smiled, the kind of smile that made you feel like everything was going to be okay. "I know it's been a while, and this might be unexpected, but I was in the area and...well, I've been thinking about you a lot lately."

Maya felt a flutter in her chest, a sensation she hadn't allowed herself to feel in so long. "Thinking about me?"

"Yes," Shaan said, stepping closer. "I know you've been through a lot, and I don't want to intrude. But I also wanted you to know that I'm here. For anything you need—whether it's a friend to talk to or someone to share a cup of coffee with."

Maya stared at the bouquet, her mind racing. She had always appreciated Shaan's steadiness, his ability to make her feel grounded even in the most chaotic moments. And now, here he was, showing up not with expectations, but with quiet support.

"Shaan...I don't know what to say," she admitted, her voice soft.

"You don't have to say anything," he replied gently. "I just wanted you to know I care. No pressure, Maya. Just...I'm here."

Her heart softened at his words. She wasn't ready for anything romantic—not yet. But there was something about Shaan's presence that felt different. It felt safe. And maybe, just maybe, she could let herself lean on that.

"Thank you," she said, a small smile forming on her lips. "That means a lot."

They spent the next hour talking—about life, work, and everything in between. For the first time in a long time, Maya felt herself relax in someone's company. Shaan didn't push her, didn't pry, and for that, she was grateful.

As he left her office, Maya watched him walk away, her thoughts swirling. She wasn't sure where this would go, but for the first time, she felt open to the possibilities. Not because she needed someone to complete her, but because she was whole enough to share herself with someone else, if and when she chose to.

What Lies Ahead

Vivhaan sat in his small, sparsely decorated apartment, the hum of the city outside barely registering in his mind. The call with Maya hadn't gone the way he'd hoped, but deep down, he knew it had gone exactly as it should have. He had hurt her in ways that couldn't be undone, and her choice to walk away from him—both then and now—was one he had to accept.

His therapist's words echoed in his mind: *"Closure doesn't come from others, Vivhaan. It comes from within. You need to learn to forgive yourself."*

But forgiving himself was harder than he had anticipated. Every day was a battle—to stay sober, to resist the pull of self-pity, to rebuild his life from the rubble he had created. His work was the one thing that gave him a sense of stability. He threw himself into it, channelling his energy into projects that demanded his full attention.

Tonight, though, the emptiness felt heavier. He scrolled through his phone absentmindedly until a notification caught his eye. It was a photo from his sister, Aarti—a candid shot of their parents laughing at a family gathering. He stared at it for a long time, a bittersweet smile tugging at his lips.

His family had stood by him through his darkest moments, but he had kept them at arm's length, too ashamed to face them fully. Maybe it was time to change that. Maybe it was time to stop isolating himself and start reconnecting with the people who had always loved him, despite everything.

Maya stood at the edge of the park, watching the sunset paint the sky in vibrant hues of orange and pink. The golden light kissed her face, and a gentle breeze carried the scent of blooming jasmine. It felt like the world itself was embracing her. For the first time in years, Maya felt truly present—rooted in the moment, unburdened by the ghosts of her past.

She thought about the conversation with Vivhaan from earlier that day. It had stirred emotions she thought she'd buried, but instead of breaking her, it had strengthened her resolve. She had spent so much time waiting for closure, for a moment where everything would make sense. But now, standing there, she realized that she didn't need anything from him anymore. She had given herself closure long ago when she chose to prioritize her well-being. Vivhaan had been a chapter of her life, but she had outgrown the story they had written together.

Her phone buzzed in her pocket, pulling her from her thoughts. It was a message from Shaan, her best friend.

Shaan: *"Where are you, woman? The party's about to start, and you're still AWOL. Do NOT make me come drag you back!"*

Maya chuckled, texting back quickly.

Maya: *"Relax, I'm on my way. Keep my cake safe!"*

*****

When Maya arrived at her house, it was alive with laughter, music, and the clinking of glasses. Balloons in pastel colors adorned the living room, and fairy lights twinkled across the walls. Her friends and family had gathered to celebrate her birthday—a day she had avoided for years because of Vivhaan. But this year was different. This year, she had decided to reclaim it.

"Finally!" Shaan exclaimed, rushing over to her with a glass of sparkling wine. "I was this close to sending a search party."

"Drama queen," Maya teased, taking the glass and hugging him tightly. "Thanks for putting all this together."

"Anything for you, birthday girl," Shaan said, grinning. "Now, go mingle. Everyone's here for *you*, and I'm not letting you sneak off to brood in a corner."

Maya laughed and was soon swept up in the warmth of the celebration. Her parents were in the kitchen, chatting with her aunt about old family stories. Her younger cousin Aisha was at the dining table, organizing a card game with her friends. And in the corner, her childhood friend Neha was playfully arguing with Shaan over the playlist.

At one point, Maya found herself surrounded by her friends, all raising their glasses in a toast.

"To Maya," Shaan declared, his voice full of emotion. "To her strength, her courage, and her absolutely terrible sense of humor. We love you, and we're so proud of the person you've become."

Maya's cheeks flushed as everyone cheered, clinking their glasses together. She looked around the room, taking in the faces of the people who had stood by her through everything. The ones who had seen her at her lowest and had celebrated every step of her journey back to herself.

Later in the evening, the moment she had dreaded—and now eagerly awaited—arrived. A massive chocolate truffle cake was brought out, candles flickering on top. As the crowd sang "Happy Birthday," Maya closed her eyes and made a wish—not for something external, but for the strength to keep choosing herself every day.

As the candles were blown out, applause erupted, and Shaan leaned over to whisper, "What did you wish for?"

"If I tell you, it won't come true," Maya teased, winking.

Epilogue

It's been more than a year since Maya walked away, and life, as unpredictable as it always is, has continued to unfold in its own beautiful, messy way.

Maya doesn't think of herself as a survivor anymore. She's more than that—she's thriving. She's rediscovered the joy of living, the thrill of laughter, and the warmth of her own company. Her world, once so clouded by darkness, now feels like a canvas painted with vibrant hues of hope and possibility.

As for Vivhaan, his chapter in her life has long since closed. Maya doesn't dwell on him anymore. Forgiveness? Maybe. Forgetting? Not entirely. But she's moved on, and that's what matters.

From what she's heard, Vivhaan is still in therapy, still fighting his demons. There are days when he stumbles, when the weight of his guilt feels too heavy to bear. But there are also days when he feels a flicker of hope, a sense that he might one day find peace. Maya doesn't wish him ill, but she knows his journey is no longer hers to carry.

From what she's heard, Vivhaan is still in therapy, still fighting his demons. There are days when he stumbles, when the weight of his guilt feels too heavy to bear. But there are also days when he feels a flicker of hope, a sense that he might one day find peace. Maya doesn't wish him ill, but she knows his journey is no longer hers to carry.

She's built a life filled with things that truly matter—friendships that nourish her soul, work that excites her, and a sense of self that no one can take away.

And love? It's not a priority. Not yet. But when it comes, she knows she'll recognize it—not by the butterflies or the fireworks, but by the peace it brings. For now, she's content in knowing that the greatest love of all is the one she's found within herself.

As for Vivhaan, his chapter in her life has long since closed. Maya doesn't dwell on him anymore. Forgiveness? Maybe. Forgetting? Not entirely. But she's moved on, and that's what matters.

If there's one thing Maya has learned, it's that life doesn't always follow the script we imagine. And that's okay. Because sometimes, the most unexpected detours lead to the most beautiful destinations.

Her story doesn't end here. It's just beginning. And she's ready—ready to write the next chapter, one day at a time, with herself as the hero of her own tale.

www.ingramcontent.com/pod-product-compliance
Lightning Source LLC
LaVergne TN
LVHW041611070526
838199LV00052B/3090